LAND OF STRANGERS

ales of the Old West. Ben Sutton is summoned exican Springs to intervene in violence that has ken out between between cattle ranchers and nesteaders. Even before he arrives, Sutton has a ly encounter with members of the Denison intent on revenge for an earlier clash. But, as n's mission is to be kept secret, he cannot information with — or even seek the nce of — the local sheriff . . . As he bivouacs Carrizo, Frank Brokaw is hopeful that his may be nearing its end. Somewhere — lly nearby — is the man who was once as Matt Slade. Brokaw doesn't know what ooks like, or the name he uses now — but he now that his quarry rides a silver-mounted and is carrying a sizeable haul of money bank robbery . . .

LAND OF STRANGERS
A WESTERN DUO

RAY HOGAN

SAGEBRUSH
Large Print Westerns

First published in the United States by Five Star

First Isis Edition
published 2017
by arrangement with
Golden West Literary Agency

A catalogue record for this book is available
from the British Library.

ISBN 978–1–78541–386–5 (pb)

Published by
F. A. Thorpe (Publishing)
Anstey, Leicestershire

Set by Words & Graphics Ltd.
Anstey, Leicestershire
Printed and bound in Great Britain by
T. J. International Ltd., Padstow, Cornwall

Contents

BEN SUTTON'S LAW 1

LAND OF STRANGERS 35

Ben Sutton's Law

CHAPTER
ONE

Ben Sutton rode into Mexican Springs around noon. He was worn, dusty, out of sorts, and there was blood on his neck as the result of an attempted ambush in rugged Navajo Cañon. Now, as he turned into the deserted street, a taut anger glowing within him, he sent his hard gaze sweeping back and forth, probing like a piercing shaft of light the passages between buildings, doorways, and windows — even the low roofs of the sun-grayed structures. They had tried to kill him once that day. No doubt they'd try again.

No one was in sight at that blisteringly hot hour, everyone apparently electing to stay well under cover for reasons of comfort, but he knew he was being watched — had been, in fact, since that moment when he had ridden out of Santa Fe. He had thought possibly the news of his mission north had been leaked, and it was still a possibility, but he gave credibility to the idea that it was some of the Denison gang, the few remaining after his encounter with them near Magdalena. They had sworn revenge and they were the sort who would never give it up.

That they were the ones who lay in wait for him in the cañon north of Taos seemed the most likely, and only that instinctive presage of danger, so thoroughly instilled in him by numberless encounters with danger, had kept him alive in those flaming moments, for small flags of warning had begun to wave inside him shortly after he forded the Río Grande and was moving onto the flat that separated the river from the black-rocked slope of the cañon to the east. Thus he had been more than half ready when the attack came. He had downed one of the four, but the others had escaped without affording him a chance to identify any of them.

His eyes picked up no suspicious movements along the way, and, spotting a livery barn across the front of which the sign *O'Hara's Stable — Horses to Rent* was boldly lettered, he angled toward it, taking note as he did of its proximity to the Chama Hotel. At the stable he swung off stiffly, and handed the hostler the reins.

"Feed him good . . . and rub him down. He's had a long day."

"Yes, sir . . . it'll be a dollar," the hostler replied, and spat brown juice into a nearby corner.

Sutton laid the coin in his hand, dropped back to the board sidewalk, and made his way to the hotel. As he crossed the porch, a man swung into the street at its far end. The rider was entering the settlement from the north, the direction opposite to that followed by him, but he slowed, nevertheless, the natural caution in him insisting that he take notice.

Standing just within the hotel's entrance, he watched the horseman pull up to O'Hara's, stop. Dismounting, he entered the sprawling building. He was gone for only two or three minutes, and then returned, swung to his

4

saddle. Glancing down the street, he wheeled around, rode back out of town, doubling over his own tracks.

Stiff, wondering, not fully satisfied, and with tension still drawing his nerves to wire tautness, Ben Sutton moved on into the shadow-filled lobby of the hotel and walked to the desk, ignoring the three or four loungers seated in the deep chairs and the solitary customer eating a midday meal in the adjoining dining area.

"Hot day," the clerk observed hopefully. He had a round face, unblinking, watery eyes, and there wasn't much hair left between him and heaven. "Come far?"

Sutton took the small pencil handed to him and bent over the register. "Not far," he murmured.

He received his key, listened to the room's number, and settled his glance on the man. He had a direct, disturbing way of looking at a person, and the clerk shifted nervously.

"Know a man around here named Whitcomb?"

The man brushed at his balding pate. "Sure . . . yes, sir. Everybody knows Amos. You looking for him?"

Ben said — "Could be." — and hesitated, his gaze settling on a girl coming through the doorway. He watched her approach, having a man's normal appreciation of her dark eyes, chestnut hair, well-developed beauty. She stopped at the desk.

"Tom . . . have you seen Yancey?"

The clerk frowned, pursed his lips. "Sure haven't. Ain't seen him for several days, in fact."

She turned away, murmuring: "He was home last night, but now . . ." Her words broke off suddenly as

she saw Sutton close by. A flush mounted her face. "I
. . . I'm sorry! I didn't mean to interrupt . . ."

"No harm done, Miss . . . Miss . . . ?"

"Murdock . . . Martha Murdock," she supplied.

He removed his hat, inclined his head courteously.
"My pleasure . . . Ben Sutton . . . at your service,
ma'am."

She smiled and for an instant the worry in her eyes
faded, and then, nodding, she wheeled about and
returned to the sidewalk.

"That brother of hers," the clerk said, wagging his
head, "he sure does worry her aplenty."

Interest stirred along different lines within Ben
Sutton as he made the connection of names —
Murdock, Yancey Murdock. That had meaning and his
thoughts went to the packet of letters inside his shirt
that contained also special authority granted to him by
the territorial governor. The girl's face blurred, receded
into the background just as had other personal
considerations in the time gone before. To Ben Sutton
the law, as always, came before all else.

"You want me to send the swamper after
Whitcomb?"

He shook his head at the clerk's offer, turned, and
made his way to his quarters — no better, no worse
than the hundreds of other hotel rooms he'd tenanted
during his life. After stripping down, he washed himself
with the tepid water standing in a china pitcher, using
the bowl that complemented it, then, propping back the
dusty curtains in the hope of finding a vagrant breeze,
he stretched out on the creaky bed for a nap.

CHAPTER
TWO

He awoke shortly after sundown, feeling much better, dressed, and went into the dining room. A half dozen patrons were there, and, touching each with a close glance, he selected a table in a corner where he had a wall to his shoulders and a complete view of the room to the front. He ordered a meal.

Half through its completion he saw an elderly man enter from the hotel's lobby, after having first paused for brief words with the clerk, and move toward him. He drew up before the table.

"You Sutton?" He had a raspy sort of voice and a nervous habit of clenching and releasing his fists as though exercising his fingers.

Ben completed the swallow of coffee he had just taken before he said: "Expect the clerk told you that. Would you be Amos Whitcomb?"

"That's me," the older man said, drawing out a chair and sitting down. Raising a hand, he motioned to the waitress for a cup of coffee, noting at that moment the welt left by the bushwhacker's bullet on Sutton's neck. "You had trouble getting here, I'd say."

"Some," the tall rider replied, sizing up Whitcomb through partly closed eyes. He recalled the governor's words: *Long-time settler in the area, owns the general store, has a finger in the bank, generally runs things in that part of the country.* That struck him as being a bit odd. If Whitcomb was such a power, why did he go to the governor for help?

"Expected you yesterday . . ."

"Late start," Sutton said. "And that ride's no Sunday picnic."

"For a fact. Howsomever, no harm done. You're here in time."

"So?"

"Word's going around . . . there'll be a raid tonight."

Ben Sutton's eyes were on the window, on three vague shadows beyond in the darkness of the street. They could be the surviving three from his encounter in Navajo Cañon just as the man he had seen ride up to O'Hara's stable might have been one of them, but he had been given no good look at any of them and so could not be sure.

"Vigilantes?"

Amos Whitcomb nodded. "Justice Committee, they call themselves. There's a homesteader upcountry a few miles. Been some beef turning up missing. They're blaming him."

"Do you?" Sutton asked, letting his eyes strike fully at the man.

Whitcomb shrugged. "Don't rightly know. Reckon you could even say I doubt it. But somebody's doing it, and there's them that's got their minds made up. Point is, what can you do about it?"

Ben settled back in his chair, threw his glance again to the street beyond the window as he fished his sack of makings out of a pocket. The three men were gone.

"My job is to do something, for sure," he said, starting a cigarette. "But I'm not certain yet just what. This homesteader . . . what's his name and how'll I find his place?"

"Bovey. Follow the river north to the buttes. You'll run right into it."

Sutton sucked his smoke into life, shook out the match, and tucked it into his vest pocket. "Do you still believe that Yancey Murdock is the head of this Justice Committee?"

Alarm spread quickly across Whitcomb's features. He glanced hurriedly about the room. "Now, I didn't say exactly that. Said it was a rumor . . . only maybe . . ."

"I see," Ben murmured. It was always the same — a man wanting a disagreeable job done but desiring no part of it himself. He guessed he'd never get used to it.

"What about your town marshal? Won't he take a hand in things?"

"Gilcrist? Don't expect nothing from him. Old . . . about all he's good for is to run in the Saturday night drunks."

"He represents the law. It ought to mean something. If he can't do that, best you make a change."

"Nobody wants the job . . . leastwise until we can sort of settle things down, nobody does."

The moments ran on, hushed yet filled with the faint rattle of pans in the restaurant's kitchen, the drone of conversation in the hotel's lobby, the slow beat of a horse's hoofs as it passed along the street. Somewhere off in the distance a church bell was tolling, summoning the faithful.

Whitcomb shifted in his chair. "Care to let me in on what you're aiming to do?"

Sutton's answer was flat. "No . . . it's a one-man circus, best to keep it that way." He paused: "One thing. Anybody here know you wrote the governor asking for me?"

"No, sir . . . nobody," the merchant insisted, his face coloring indignantly. "You think I . . . ?"

"Not thinking anything special," Sutton broke in. "Just wondering about things."

Whitcomb shrugged, got to his feet. He brushed at the sweat on his cheeks, shoved his chair back into place. "You want me, you know where I'll be . . . my store," he said, and, turning on his heel, he cut back through the hotel lobby.

A bit later Ben saw him pass into the street, bending his steps for the wide, long, running porch that fronted his establishment. Amos Whitcomb was a man not too difficult to understand; he was simply looking out for his own best interests.

The merchant disappeared in the blackness of his building, and almost immediately Ben saw a man come from the marshal's office, cross the street at a leisurely pace. He was well up in years, his trailing mustache and shoulder-length hair now a snow white, but he carried himself erectly, as if wanting one and all to see the star he wore pinned to the pocket of his vest. He'd been the

10

town's marshal for twenty years or more — and his time was past but it was not in the man ever to admit it.

A stir of pride moved through Ben Sutton, as it always did when he encountered one of the old lawmen still going about his task. These were the fellows all settlements were indebted to, for they were the ones who laid their lives on the line every hour of the day and night just so a man and his wife could walk down a street, or their children could go safely to school. But only too often, as the case appeared here, they were forgotten, relegated, as an old horse might be, to the pasture of meaningless, harmless chores.

He watched Gilcrist come through the doorway, make his survey of the now almost empty dining room, and then move up to his table and halt. Despite the heat, the lawman wore his shirt sleeves cuffed and a string tie closing the collar.

"'Evening," he said. "Don't recollect seeing you around before."

"Rode in about noon," Sutton replied agreeably.

He was studying the marshal, not sure if this was the usual, casual inquiry of a town's lawman checking on a new arrival, or if it went further than that. Gilcrist could have seen him talking with Whitcomb and was now on a fishing expedition, or his appearance shortly after the merchant had departed could be just coincidence. He wished he could invite the man to sit down, talk things over with him, ask a few questions that he needed to be answered — but that was out. A man doing the job assigned to him must necessarily work alone. To ask one question of an outsider that related to the matter under attention might arouse suspicion and undo weeks, even months, of hard work. That was one of the things that all too often disheartened Ben Sutton — that eternal, lone-wolf way of life.

"Aim to be around long?"

"Hard to say, Marshal."

Gilcrist drew out a bandanna, mopped at his craggy features. "Just one thing I've got to say . . . I'm running a peaceful town. Want to keep it that way. You got other ideas, you'd best mount up and ride on."

"You'll get no trouble from me," Ben said. "It seems I've heard other things about your town, though . . . about how . . ."

"You're talking about what's going on in the valley. That's got nothing to do with my town."

Words to the contrary came swiftly to Sutton's lips, but he held them back. It was pointless to get in an argument with Gilcrist who seemed determined simply to turn his back on everything outside the town's limits — and there was that danger of tipping his own hand, arousing suspicion that could cause complications.

"Glad to hear that, Marshal," he said, rising and dropping some coins on the table to pay for his meal. "Town's quiet . . . always a good sign."

Lon Gilcrist bobbed his head, smiled briefly, and turned away. Sutton watched him leave, and, when the lawman was again visible in the street, he moved back into the lobby and went to his room. He stood by the window for a full hour, gazing on the street, wondering about the three men he had noticed, and then quietly left his quarters, followed out the hall to the rear door, and let himself into the alley that ran behind the building.

Halting there in the darkness, he waited until his eyes were fully adjusted to the change in light and he was certain that no one was close by. Then he hurried to O'Hara's where he stood by silently while the hostler saddled and bridled the roan.

"You'll be coming back?" the overalled man asked as he led the gelding into the runway.

"I'll be back," Sutton answered, swinging to the saddle. *Anyway, I'm hoping to*, he added silently as he walked the horse out into the open.

He rode northward for the Bovey place, keeping out of sight as much as possible, carefully circling the ranch houses and other homesteaders that were *en route*. Now and then something within the man checked him and he would hesitate and listen for any sounds of pursuit — and once he circled wide, cut back for a good half mile before he was completely satisfied that there was no one on his trail.

Such precaution was second nature with Ben Sutton. He took a few minutes, always aware that in his line of work one small mistake could be his last, and now, as he drifted quietly and steadily along through the night, seeing the friendly lights of different homes along the way, it came to him that, actually, it was a hell of a way to live — and what a fine thing it would be to have a place of his own and a wife waiting for him at sundown. A wife such as Martha Murdock . . .

He shifted on the saddle, a little surprised and somewhat disturbed that she should find a place in his thoughts. But she was there and he found himself remembering how she looked and the sound of her voice and the way sunlight had danced upon her hair when she stepped out into the open. The thought was not good; likely when Martha learned his identity and purpose, she would only think the worst of him.

It would be a fine thing to settle down, and of late the idea had been coming into his mind more and more. Could he do it? Could he really live like other men? That question, too, had entered his consideration. What would it be like not to be forever on the move, not following out some outlaw's trail, not climbing an endless hill or riding fast across a wide, flat mesa in a desperate effort to ward off trouble?

What would it feel like to walk down the street of a town without viewing every passer-by with suspicion? How would it seem never again to have trouble bending overhead like a dark, threatening cloud, or feel the weight of a gun on your hip and the pressure of a cartridge belt around your belly? Would he ever know?

Deep within him were strong doubts. He had no illusions about himself, his job, or the ruthless nature of the men with whom he was compelled to deal. Somewhere along the line there was always and inevitably a man who got lucky or who was able to draw his pistol and get off a shot just a trace faster. Such was as certain as darkness followed daylight — and the smart ones bore that in mind and got out in time.

He'd do that, too. He had meant to all along. So far, however, the time just hadn't shaped up to where it was possible. Mainly — the law wasn't ready. He wouldn't turn in his special officer badge yet — not until he was certain in his own mind that the regularly constituted lawmen could handle any and all problems that arose.

CHAPTER
THREE

He topped out on a grassy knoll, looked down upon the Bovey place. It lay in a wide field that backed against a small creek, flowing like a strip of polished silver through the moonlight. It was a small homestead, of the type that cattlemen hated but that would someday sprinkle the country, and Sutton, viewing the ramshackle buildings moodily, thought: *Even he's got more than I've got.*

As he watched, the yellow square of light in a window blanked out. Bovey had retired. Urging the roan forward at a slow walk, he descended the slope and pulled to a stop next to a slab shed, pleased that no dogs had heard or seen him and set up their racket.

He sat quietly in the saddle, a lonely man doing a lonely thing, and let his mind stray. Around him in the night were all the pleasant, earthy smells of a farm, the muted, satisfying noises of livestock in the barn. Far off in the hills to the east a coyote barked, and once there was the swish of broad, set wings as a hunting owl passed swiftly by. Unexpectedly the roan blew, stamped. Sutton came up sharply, tense, afraid someone inside the house had heard and would appear, but the place remained dark, and he settled back, relieved.

And then, from the south, came the drumming tattoo of fast-running horses. At once all else faded from Ben Sutton's mind, and, slipping from the roan, he drew up close to the shed near which he waited, listening intently. At least a half dozen riders, he guessed, possibly more. Shortly the drumming ceased as if a halt had been called, but he realized they had simply pulled down to a walk in order to deaden the noise of their coming.

When at last they came into sight, he saw there were ten men in all, each wearing a head mask of white cloth that hung to their shoulders and lending them a ghostly, square face with round, empty eyes. They ranged up before the Bovey place in a shallow half circle, and the leader, advancing a few steps, drew his gun. The sound exploded into the night, setting off a chain of echoes.

Almost at once a light blossomed inside the structure, and Sutton, moving silently, eased forward in the shadows until he stood at the corner of the house. In the next moment the door creaked and the homesteader, a ludicrous figure in a long, white nightshirt, lamp held overhead, came out into the yard. He stared at the line of riders and then, voice pitched in alarm, cried: "Vigilantes!"

"Bovey," the leader said, "appears we've made a mistake."

"Mistake? How . . . what's that mean?"

"We shouldn't've let you and your kind ever squat in this country. For cattle . . . not sodbustin' . . ."

"But we're down here in the valley. Ain't no cattle raising done along here. We ain't bothering you none."

"You're helping yourself to our beef sure is," another of the masked men cut in harshly. "Got to stop."

"I ain't never touched any of your stock . . . before God, I swear it!"

"We know better, Bovey. Now, get your woman and young 'uns out of that shack . . . we're burning it down."

Sutton, anger rising swiftly within him, moved forward. Hand resting on the butt of the gun, he threw his flat voice into the sudden hush.

"This stops right here!"

Bovey wheeled, startled by his appearance. The vigilante leader struggled with his horse briefly while behind him a mutter of words broke out. At once the night became tense.

"Who the hell are you, mister?"

Ben Sutton moved farther into the open. In the pale light his face was a cold, expressionless mask. "Makes no difference who I am . . . point is, you're not the law. If you've got any complaints against this man, take them to the marshal or the nearest sheriff."

One of the masked men laughed. "Can see he's a stranger . . . telling us to go to Gilcrist!"

The vigilante leader nodded. "That's right . . . we're the only law around here . . . we've got to be. Marshal don't amount to a hill of beans."

"He still represents the law . . . and it's up to you to respect it. Something you . . . all of you . . . better get straight. This is a territory of the United States. It's under civil government, and there's no room in it for masked riders running around taking matters into their own hands."

"Government . . . hell! What good's that? Where was the god-damned government when we needed some help? Where was it when that wild bunch from Colorado rode in here and raided our herds? Where was it when the Jenson gang come sashaying through here, shooting up everything . . . and killing my pa and ma? I'll tell you where, Mister Buttinsky . . . setting on their tails in Santa Fe, doing nothing!"

A sigh passed through Ben Sutton. The minds of men worked in direct, bitter ways; always they justified their acts of vengeance by misguided thoughts of personally meted out justice that had its birth in some terrible experience that warped and soured them beyond reason. He could understand their desire, but he could not condone it. Such was the purpose of the law.

And he knew now for sure who the leader of the vigilantes — the Justice Committee as they called themselves — actually was: Yancey Murdock. It had been his parents the Jenson bunch had senselessly murdered.

"And what about the Gilpins? They sure didn't get no help when . . ."

"All right, all right," Sutton broke in. "That's all in the past. This is right now, and things've changed. Like

19

I said, if you have something to charge this man with, go to the marshal, tell him."

"And if we don't want to do it that way?"

"Then you've got trouble on your hands. I'm an officer of the law, special . . . out of the governor's office. You try going ahead and you've got me to crawl over."

"It won't be no chore," one of the men said. "The odds are plenty our way."

"Maybe . . . but there'll be six of you who won't see the sun come up. I'll get that many of you before I'm finished."

Murdock was leaning forward on his saddle. "Somebody send for you?" he asked in a suspicious voice. "One of these squatters, maybe?"

"No," Ben said flatly, and dropped it there. "Now, what's it to be? We're handling this the way it's supposed to be, a trial for this man before a judge and jury . . . or is there to be bloodshed? The choice is yours. You figure you . . ."

Ben Sutton's words broke off as a warning shot through him. His ears picked up the faintest of sounds. Instinctively he dodged to one side, started to wheel. In the next fragment of time something solid crashed into his head and he went spinning down into a black void.

CHAPTER
FOUR

He seemed to be fighting his way upward, out of a deep pit. He felt a cool cloth touch his forehead, and, as the veil of cobwebs tore, began to fade from his mind, he heard Bovey's voice.

"Just you rest easy, mister . . . you're going to be all right."

He stirred impatiently, tried to rise. Pain, in a shocking wave, struck him. He sank back once again, descended into the darkness.

He opened his eyes much later. It was near dawn, and he could hear a rooster crowing proudly nearby. He was inside the homesteader's, lying on a corn-shuck mattress placed on a crudely made bed. Bovey and a worn-looking woman with stringy hair were looking down at him. He sat up slowly as if testing each inch. There was little pain although his head ached. Pivoting, he threw his legs over the edge of the bed.

"Stay right there," the homesteader said then. "The wife'll get you a cup of coffee . . . what you're needing."

Sutton murmured his assent. A stiff shot of whiskey would be more to the heart of things, but he made no mention of it and accepted the thick crockery cup of steaming liquid, downed it.

"Obliged to you," he said, nodding to the woman, and then turned his eyes to Bovey. "You see who hit me?"

The homesteader shook his head. "Never seen hardly anything. There you was standing there, next thing I knowed you was falling . . ."

Sutton swore silently. He had failed. Oh, sure, he had prevented the night riders from burning down the Bovey place, but that was secondary to his way of thinking. Where he had failed was in proving the strength and invincibility of organized law.

"You think it was one of those masked men?" he asked, rising. He made the move too quickly, was forced to stand motionless, eyes clasped shut, while a wave of nausea rolled through him.

"No, sir, don't figure it was. Can't figure out why, but I think it was somebody else altogether. And them vigilantes, they was about as surprised as me."

The unsteadiness passed. Ben opened his eyes, found Mrs. Bovey standing beside him, another cup of coffee in her hand. Her colorless lips parted into a smile of sorts.

"I'd be right pleased to fix you something to eat. Got some bacon and eggs . . . or maybe you'd want . . ."

"Coffee's doing the job fine," Sutton said, and again thanked her.

His mind was clearing rapidly now, functioning as it should despite the dull aching. He had his own doubts, too, where his attacker was concerned. He would have noticed one of the riders moving away, circling to get in behind him, and the entire group had pulled up in front of Bovey's, with no thought given to encircling the place. No, it was someone else, an outsider. Who? It occurred to him then that the only other person who would know that he intended to be at Bovey's that night was Amos Whitcomb.

At that realization all conjecture and speculation came to a halt on dead center. Whitcomb! It didn't make sense — yet, perhaps it did. But it actually didn't matter for the moment, anyway. It was a side issue, one to be fathomed out later. The important thing was that he knew the leader of the masked men — the Justice Committee — who were riding the hills, terrorizing all with their kind of law, and that was the key to the situation he had been directed to correct.

"Where's the Murdock Ranch from here?" he asked, moving toward the door.

"About ten mile west," Bovey answered. He bent forward, peered closely at Ben. "You sure you're up to riding, mister? Maybe you ought to wait . . ."

"I'm fine . . . that my hat over there on the table?"

The homesteader reached for Sutton's headgear, passed it to him. A frown clouded his face. "About all that fuss last night . . . ain't you even going to ask if I done what they claimed . . . stole that beef?"

"It's not my business to ask," Sutton replied, "only to see that you get a fair hearing in a court if somebody wants to charge you with it. I'm interested in the law being used right . . . nothing else."

The homesteader bobbed his head. "Well, I'm mighty thankful you was here. My old woman and me and the kids'd sure be out in the cold right now if you hadn't . . . and maybe it'd've been worse. They've done strung up a couple or so they claimed was rustling . . . caught them at it, they said. And then they burned down the Ellermyers' and the Simpsons', drove them clean out of the country."

"A body just ain't safe!" Mrs. Bovey wailed suddenly from the kitchen. "I ain't staying around here no longer . . . and that's the gospel."

"It'll be safe from here on," the homesteader said. "We're going to have a good law now. Folks'll be able to go about their business and not be scared."

"Ain't going to make no difference! Between them there cattlemen and gangs like them Jensons, decent folks can't . . ."

Sutton stepped out into the yard, waited on the sagging stoop while one of Bovey's older children led the roan to him, smiled shyly, and hurried away. Shoving his toe into the stirrup, Ben swung onto the saddle. The homesteader moved up beside him, his face sober.

"Mister, I'm mighty grateful for what you done, and I'm saying it again. Now, is there something that you're wanting me to do to sort of straighten things out with this law you're fixing to put in here?"

"Not putting it in . . . it's already here and has been since General Kearney came through nearly thirty years ago. People in this part of the territory have just ignored it. You want to do right by it, go into town and talk to the marshal. Tell him you've been accused of cattle rustling and you want either to be tried before a judge for it . . . or you want the people accusing you of it to shut up and make you an apology."

Bovey stared. "Them cattle growers . . . apologize to me?"

"It's what they'll have to do . . . unless they're right."

The homesteader drew himself up stiffly. "Well, they sure ain't right, I never stoled nothing in my life." He bobbed his head decisively. "All right, mister, I'll do it. I'm going in and talk to the marshal today."

"It's the right thing to do," Ben Sutton said, smiling, and rode out of the yard.

He traveled leisurely in the warm morning sunshine, pointing due west, letting the roan choose his way while he mulled over the events of the last hours in his mind. Few things were making sense, other than the fact that he knew definitely the identity of the Justice Committee's leader, and that was, after all, most important. But who, if not one of their members, would wish to stop him? That it could be Amos Whitcomb didn't seem logical; neither did it seem likely that it was one of the men who had attempted to ambush him. They would not have wasted their time on simply knocking him unconscious — their intent was to kill.

The solution to that lay in the future — after he had settled with Yancey Murdock, which was now at hand, he realized, as the road turned sharply into a wide, cottonwood-shaded yard in which stood a cluster of well-tended, neatly painted buildings that immediately brought to him the thought: *This is the kind of place I'd like to have*.

Walking the gelding up to the hitch rack where two horses stood, hip-slacked, he stepped down. The sweet smell of honeysuckle hung in the clean air, and he had hesitated, motionless, caught up by that when the screen door of the house opened and Martha Murdock came out onto the porch to greet him.

"Why, it's Mister Sutton," she said, pleased. "It's nice of you to drop by."

He nodded, fumbled off his hat while a strange, disturbing sensation coursed through him, turning him awkward, thickening his tongue. He murmured something in reply, checked himself, grateful for the appearance of Yancey Murdock in that exact moment. The young rancher emerged from the office he maintained at the lower end of the gallery, eying Ben coldly.

"What's on your mind?" he asked in a hostile voice.

Martha turned to her brother in surprise. "Oh, you know each other?"

"Some," Yancey said, and waited for Sutton to answer.

Ben shrugged. He preferred to discuss matters in private, particularly not in front of Martha, but Murdock seemed not to care.

"I'm here about last night," he said. "Do you think having one of your bunch hit me over the head would make any difference?"

"I had nothing to do with that," the rancher said sharply. "I don't know who it was . . . and he was gone before we could find out."

Sutton had guessed that was the way of it, but he wanted to be certain. He glanced at the girl, and almost regretfully said: "I'm serving notice on you, Murdock ... officially ... you're to disband this vigilante committee you're leading. Time for that kind of thing is over ... finished."

From the tail of his eye Ben saw Martha stiffen, move to her brother's side. Evidently she knew of the masked men.

Yancey shook his head. "All right, you've given me the notice. It means nothing. We'll still have to look after things up here."

"No ... it's done with. Maybe there was a time when it was necessary, but no longer. The law will take care of any such problems."

"Law," Murdock echoed scornfully. "What law? That old man down in town that's wearing a badge? That what you mean by the law?"

"He represents the law," Sutton said quietly, "and maybe, if you and your masked avengers had gotten with him and backed him up when things started going wrong ... he'd be the law. But you took it on yourselves, instead. All right, if that's what the problem is, I'll see that you get a new marshal ... a tough one who'll handle things to suit even you."

Yancey Murdock frowned. "We don't want no gunslinger running around here loose."

"What do you think you and your committee are? You're even worse ... jumping at rumors, punishing a man when you don't know anything for sure ... hanging, murdering just because you think you're right.

27

A hired gun, at least, usually knows for sure why he kills."

Martha's hand was on her brother's arm. "Yancey . . . maybe he's right. Maybe you should let the law . . ."

The sharp, flat crack of a rifle sliced through her words. In that same fraction of an instant Ben Sutton felt a bullet tug at his sleeve, whirled. Three men on horses were silhouetted on a ridge only yards away. The last of the Denison gang — he recognized one of them this time. He'd been right. They had dogged his trail ever since Magdalena, had made their try in Navajo Cañon, failed, and were here now to settle it once and for all — claim their vengeance or die in the attempt.

"Get Martha inside!" he yelled at Murdock, and, drawing his pistol, started zigzagging up the slope that led to where the riders had halted.

"I'll get my gun . . . give you a hand!" Yancey shouted, grasping the girl's arm, rushing her toward the house.

"No . . . this is my problem . . . the law's!" Sutton yelled back without slowing. "I'll take care of it!"

He heard Yancey make some sort of reply as he pressed on, but he did not catch the words. The Denisons were firing steadily at him but his erratic course and their own nervous horses were making accuracy impossible. He plunged on, holding back his return fire until he was in better range, feeling the muscles of his legs beginning to tighten under the strain of running uphill, his breathing to grow more difficult.

A bullet ripped across his arm, tearing through the sleeve of his shirt, slicing a groove in the skin. He paused then, aimed at the man nearest him, squeezed off a shot. The rider threw up his arms, falling sideways from his saddle. Cool, ignoring another bullet plucking at his leg, Ben Sutton leveled his weapon at the man in the center, triggered his weapon. The outlaw buckled forward, tumbling to the sandy ground. Sutton threw himself to one side then, wanting to offer no better target. Motion to his far left sent a warning through him — two riders coming along the road. He swore softly, threw himself full length, pistol leveled at the last man on the ridge.

Surprise and relief rolled through him. The rider had dropped his weapon to the ground, had raised his hands above his head in a sign of surrender. Immediately Sutton transferred his attention to the approaching men — and again heaved a sigh. It was Bovey, the homesteader, and with him was Marshal Lon Gilcrist.

Ben got to his feet, motioned to the man on the ridge who rode forward slowly, starting down the slope. When he drew abreast, Sutton said — "Get off . . . walk." — and, when the man complied, followed him down into Murdock's yard where Bovey and Gilcrist were joining Martha and Yancey.

"Your prisoner," Sutton said to the old lawman, shoving the outlaw toward him. "I'll be in, make out the charges."

Gilcrist dug a pair of chain-linked cuffs from his saddlebags, put them about the man's wrists, then handed the key to Ben. "Maybe you won't be wanting me to, after you hear what I've got to say."

Sutton looked at the marshal more closely. On beyond him, he could see Martha smiling at him proudly, could hear Yancey telling Bovey and several of the ranch hands who had been attracted by the gunshots of the incident: "Damnedest thing I ever saw. Them three lined up there on that ridge, shooting at him . . . and him charging them like he was the whole U.S. Cavalry! If that's the kind of law . . ."

"I'm listening," Sutton said to the lawman.

Gilcrist squared his thin shoulders. "It was me that hit you over the head last night."

Sutton drew up in surprise. Yancey Murdock and the others fell silent, equally startled.

"You . . . why?" Ben demanded in a tight voice.

"I knew what you'd come to Mexican Springs for. Got it from a deputy in Santa Fe . . . said the governor was sending you to straighten things out . . . figured I knew, I reckon, me being the marshal."

"Why didn't you speak up when we were talking? I'd have brought you in on it if I thought you knew."

"Didn't know just what I ought to be doing. Anyway, I followed you out to Bovey's, and, when it looked like you was about to take over, force the committee to quit, I stepped in."

"Why . . . I'll ask it again?" Sutton pressed.

"Good reason . . . knowed that I couldn't handle things alone, but long as the Justice Committee kept riding the hills, outlaw gangs like the Jensons and rustlers and such would stay clear of us. It was the only

30

way I could see to keep law and order. Your just coming up here once, then pulling out, leaving us, won't help none."

A surge of anger rolled through Ben Sutton. This was the sort of thing he had to fight — this selfishness, this single-minded kind of personal law — this type of self-preservation. And then he felt a wave of pity.

He was wrong to condemn lawmen such as Lon Gilcrist. In number they were pitifully few when compared to the outlaws they were forced to contend with — and all worked under great odds, quite often bucked strong opposition from the very people they sought to protect. He should not blame Lon Gilcrist for taking advantage of any and every opportunity for holding the lawless element at bay.

"Well, I don't think we'll be needing the Justice Committee any longer," Yancey Murdock said, stepping up beside the old lawman and laying an arm across his shoulder. "And I don't figure you need to worry none about keeping things peaceful . . . not if that's the kind of law Sutton's talking about."

Ben nodded. "It is . . . the kind that handles the outlaws without folks taking things into their own hands."

Gilcrist shook his head. "Just . . . just don't see how I can . . . alone."

"You're not alone. Every town in the territory's got or will have a good, honest lawman."

"But I'm getting old and . . ."

"It makes no difference. The point is the people will stand behind you . . . and that's what makes the law . . .

people backing up the man they elected to wear a star. With that happening all over the country, the day of the outlaw will soon pass."

"Amen to that," Bovey murmured.

Yancey Murdock nodded briskly to Gilcrist. "I can see what he means, Marshal . . . and you'll get your backing up from here on. I'll see to it." He paused, turned to Sutton. "Big county, howsomever, and we don't have a sheriff right now. Job's open to you if you want it. I know other ranchers and homesteaders would be for it. Or maybe you'd like to get a place of your own . . . raise cattle . . ."

Ben stared off across the smooth hills, remembering all the things he'd like to do, to have, remembering, too, the endless days, the lonely nights, fully aware in those moments of Martha, standing at the edge of the porch, her eyes bright with promise, lips parted in a hopeful smile — a life with her, a ranch of his own. Peace, the end of danger, of trouble, of loneliness.

And then he had a quick realization of that worn, harried man in the Governor's Palace in Santa Fe, with all his great plans for the territory, and he thought of all the other Lon Gilcrists needing help, struggling to make the badge they wore mean something — and he knew that it could never be. The law was a part of him — a second heart, perhaps — and he would be duty-bound and forever obligated to serve it until one day it could stand alone, unassisted, and not be challenged.

He did not look at Martha, but simply nodded to Yancey and said: "I'm obliged for the offer, but I reckon

I'd better keep working at what I'm doing." Moving to his horse, he went to the saddle, settled himself, threw his attention to Gilcrist.

"Marshal, I expect we'd better get the prisoner to your jail. Then I'd best be on my way."

Gilcrist motioned the last of the Denisons to his mount, climbed onto his own horse. Yancey Murdock stepped forward, extended his hand to Ben.

"I'd like you to know there'll always be a place at our table for you."

Sutton smiled. "I appreciate that . . . and maybe someday I'll just drop by." Only then did he raise his eyes to meet those of Martha. "*Adiós*," he said softly, and, wheeling the roan about, rode out of the yard.

LAND OF STRANGERS

CHAPTER
ONE

Spring was having her wild, young way in the bottom land along the Carrizo. Like a woman preening herself for the Saturday night dance in town, she was putting forth her best, wiping away the chill memories of winter's bitter sojourn, brushing warmness and life into the willows and dogbush, the crisp grass and gaunt cottonwoods, and even the crackling mesquite. The hostile wind with its fierce, slashing drive was gentle now, bringing the smells of greening things from the north where lay the towering Pass country, and from the west, where the ragged edges of the Sierra Diablos etched their crags against the horizon.

In the thick brush shaping up along the rumbling stream, Frank Brokaw had laid his night camp. Squatting now on his heels in the half dawn, he waited for coffee to come to a boil, mechanically feeding dry twigs into the small fire. He was a sun-blackened, young man with a face too old for his years. The coffee lifted to a foaming crest and he set the lard tin aside. With the blade of his pocket knife he stirred down the froth, waited for it to cool, and then tipped the small bucket to his mouth and drank until there was nothing left but the sack of grounds.

How long had he been on the trail? Almost a year now. Almost a year following a stone-cold trail, hunting a man he did not know and had never seen. And a nameless man at that. Matt Slade he had called himself back in Central City where the explosion, and all the other things had taken place. But it would not be that now. A man doing what Matt Slade had done would be quick to change his name.

Reaching into an inner pocket for tobacco and papers, he deftly spun up a brown cigarette. With the glowing end of a brand from the dying fire, he lit it, sucked deeply of the smoke, and rose to his feet — throwing his glance out across the brightening landscape.

Grass rolled away in all four directions, in hazy silver-tinged brown waves, reaching even to the savage black edges of the badlands — *malpais* he had heard it called. The Carrizo twisted northerly in a glistening, irregular band. The river was deep, not yet at flood point, but it would become so when the snows in the high country felt the bite of the sun and began melting. Then the water would come rushing down to overflow the stream's banks and spread out into shallow lakes on the flats. That was the way of this strange land. Always an overabundance. Always too much of one thing: too much wind, too much snow, too much sun and heat, too much cold. A world of extremes.

But it was a strong country, one that appealed deeply to him, and he had a lonely man's brief wish that he might call it his own, that he might settle down on its lush, inviting contours and carve out a home for himself. But instead, he reflected grimly, he was bringing violence to it. He would find no friends in this land of strangers. And he would likely leave none.

Eight years ago it had been different. The war was but a distant, threatening grumble, a far call from the farm of his parents in eastern Kansas, where one day was much like another, and a boy could find his happiness in everything he did, and his dreams in every cloud he saw. Then came Fort Sumter, and the roil of summoning drums spreading their call to the remotest points. Frank Brokaw was seventeen when he joined up.

Four years later it was all over. Sick of blood and vowing never again to lift a gun, unable to get the smell of death from his nostrils, he became a footloose drifter. He saw all of Texas. He rode deep into Mexico. He crossed the bottom of New Mexico Territory and passed through the new one called Arizona. He saw the Pacific's waters from California's shores, turned inland across the glittering deserts, and came finally back to Kansas, four years later.

There, everything had changed. Eight years had made a difference and the world he had known was gone. People he never saw before occupied the little farm. His mother was dead, gone of a broken heart they said. His father, a kindly man, loved and respected by all as town marshal, was a hopeless, mindless dead man alive, languishing in the Home for the Insane at Leavenworth. And a man called Matt Slade, responsible for those changes, had disappeared into the vast reaches of the West.

Brokaw dropped the cold cigarette into the ashes of his fire and ground it out. With the toe of a boot he raked moist earth over the embers and trod the dark scar into a mound. He had saddled and loaded his remaining grub on the bay gelding while the coffee had brewed, and now moved toward the big horse, walking in that easy, muscular, swinging way of a man confident of his powers.

He was a tall man, not heavy, but not thin, either. His hips were narrow, pinched in at the waist, giving him a sort of wedge-shape torso with wide-flung shoulders. He wore the usual range variety of clothing: coarse shirt faded to a light mouse color, sun-bleached Levi's, dust- and alkali-stained boots, a wide-brimmed hat that had seen better days. An old, bone-handled Colt revolver, his father's, sagged from a belt around his waist, and his spurs were those of a cavalryman.

His face was broad, hard-cornered, placid, tanned to the depths of muddy water. His mouth was long, his nose prominent, and his eyes were yellow-hazel beneath a shelf of heavy, black brows. Like a dark shadow a measure of cynicism, of arrogance, lay across his features and pulsed through the seemingly careless, but sure movements of him, as he stalked to the bay.

He stowed the lard bucket in the left-hand side of the saddlebags, taking time to thread all three buckles. That done, he checked the double cinches of the old work saddle. He found them to his satisfaction and swung aboard, going up in an easy, fluid motion. For a moment he sat quietly staring out over the smooth, undulating plains to the west. Far to his right, up a long distance and near the Carrizo, a wisp of pale smoke lifted into the morning sky, marking a ranch or a homesteader, grubbing out a tough living from a quarter section. Or, perhaps, the camp of a solitary man like himself. He would not be going that way. He was striking on west, to a ranch called the Arrowhead and a man named Hugh Preston. Maybe this last tip would prove right. Maybe this would be the end of the trail and Hugh Preston would be, in reality, the man who had called himself Matt Slade.

Preston, they had said in Tascosa, had moved into the Scattered Hills country five or six years back. That would be about the right time. He had bought up a run-down spread belonging to a man named Cresswell. He had paid for it with hard cash money. And then had rebuilt it, stocking it well with cattle bought wherever and whenever available. And always paying cash. That fitted, too. Matt Slade would have plenty of cash.

He clucked the bay into motion and turned him up the gentle incline leading from the stream. That was when he heard the first, fading roll of gunfire.

CHAPTER
TWO

Instantly alert and curious, as any man would be, he jerked the bay to a halt. The shots seemed to have come from his left, from beyond a low ridge lying parallel to the trail he had taken. But sounds fool a man in wide, open country, and so he waited. A minute later they came again, three quick reports flatting hollowly in the clear air.

Sure of his bearings now, he spurred the gelding to a gallop, striking for the highest point of the ridge a half mile off. The bay horse, fresh from the night's rest on good graze and water, strung out swiftly, gaining the crest in long, easy strides. Brokaw checked there, having to hold the bay, that wanted to continue the run, with a tight rein. He found himself on the rim of a shallow basin that swooped away for a good five miles before him.

Two hundred yards distant stood a canvas-topped wagon apparently halted in its eastward course across the range. Two riders sat their saddles, their opposed ropes suspending between them a man in rough, butternut clothing, pinning him like a calf about to be branded. Their guns were out and they were lacing the ground about the man's feet with bullets, all the while commanding him to dance.

Brokaw studied the scene with no outward change of expression, its meaning coming quickly to him. A transient homesteader caught on cattle land. It had happened many times before. The riders would rough him up a bit, scare him half to death, and then warn him to move on. But in the end no real harm would be done. He turned back for the trail. It was no affair of his and there was no call for him to butt in.

His swinging glance caught sight of another rider then, coming in from the south. A distant blur, he was riding hard, attracted also by the gunshots, Brokaw guessed. The homesteader at that moment was down, struggling fiercely. Both cowpunchers were laughing as their horses backed away, pulling tight the ropes.

A voice floated up to Brokaw: "Let's build a fire and brand him!"

Another sound reached him. The shrill, faint scream of a woman. He spun the bay around and spurred along the ridge, running hard for a good quarter mile. From a point reached by that action, he could see the front of the wagon. A third horse, hidden from him before by the vehicle's bulk, waited near a front wheel. A thick-bodied man wrestled with a woman, the homesteader's wife likely, on the seat. Brokaw flung a quick glance at the approaching horseman. Still a long way off. And he might be a friend of the three cowboys, anyway. Settling his hat with a hard pulling of the brim, he spoke to the bay and they went racing down the long slope.

The woman's screams became louder as he drew nearer. He quartered in, keeping the wagon between himself and the two riders with the ropes. But the drum of the bay's hoofs brought the man on the seat half around. He let his hands fall away from the woman's body, mouth sagging a little with surprise. Brokaw swung in close. He reached out with one hand, caught the man by the arm, lost his grip, and clutched at the loose cloth of his brush jacket. The sudden shock almost pulled his arm from its socket, but he hung on and the man came hurtling off the wagon.

"Look out, Shep!" one of the cowpunchers yelled belatedly.

Brokaw spun the bay around, dragging out his gun. He snapped a shot at the closest rider. "Throw down those ropes!"

Both cowboys complied instantly. The homesteader scrambled to his feet, kicked out of the ropes, and lunged for the old Sharps rifle lying near the wagon where he had dropped it. Through all the whirling confusion the woman's voice shrilled on hysterically.

Brokaw heard a growl behind him and remembered the man he had catapulted from the wagon. He tried to wheel away, but hands seized his arm and dragged him from the saddle. He struck hard, losing his gun and hat, and the bay went shying off a dozen feet. He forgot the other two men as the third, Shep by name apparently, began hammering at him with huge fists. The homesteader's rifle blasted suddenly, setting up a chain of echoes, but he could not turn to see if the man had hit one of the cowboys. He rolled, going over and over, getting away from Shep.

The rifle thundered again. One of the riders yelled. Brokaw got his feet under him and bounded up. He saw the two cowpunchers standing with their arms over their heads under the wavering barrel of the homesteader's gun. On beyond them, the rider from the south hove into view, his gray horse moving at a long lope. He would be there shortly, and, if he was a friend of the trio, Brokaw realized he would be in a bad spot. He would have to finish this quickly.

Shep rushed in and he met the cowboy with a sharp right to the jaw. It rocked the man back and Brokaw crowded in, driving him to his heels with a rapid tattoo of rights and lefts. Shep stumbled away, turning about. Brokaw followed closely. The cowpuncher, finally regaining his balance, pivoted fast, for a big man. He lashed out with a swinging, backhanded blow. It caught Brokaw across the neck, grazing his chin, not hurting much, but stalling him temporarily. Before he could duck and weave away, a hard right caught him, and set lights to dancing in front of his eyes.

"Get him, Shep!" one of the riders yelled.

Brokaw slid away from the next broad swing, letting it skip off his shoulder. It threw Shep again off balance when it missed, and he took a stumbling step forward. Brokaw, his head clear once more, allowed him to reel by. Shep was wide open. Brokaw, with a terrific, down-sledging blow to the side of the head, dropped him flat.

He stepped away, sucking deep for wind. Legs spread wide, knotted fists poised, he waited for Shep to rise again.

"Reckon that'll be about enough," a voice drawled through the hush.

Brokaw lifted his gaze to the speaker. The man on the gray horse. He sat forward in the saddle, both hands resting on the horn. He was an old man, his long hair and trailing handlebar mustache full white, and startlingly offset by jet black, bushy brows. His eyes were a keen blue reaching out authoritatively from a ruddy, hawk-like face. Sunlight glinted sharply off the star pinned to his vest pocket.

Brokaw turned deliberately away, placing his shoulders to the lawman, waiting for Shep to regain his feet. It would be over if Shep said so, if Shep had had enough, and not because a man with a tin badge said it should be. He was poised, ready, willing to carry on the battle if necessary.

"Don't you go turnin' your back on me, mister!" the sheriff barked. "I said this ruckus was over and I mean just that! You try carryin' it further and I'll put a bullet in your leg!"

Brokaw made no sign he had heard. He watched Shep get to his hands and knees, head hanging like a bushed horse. He watched him shake himself and climb slowly to his feet and pivot tiredly around. Blood streaked from a corner of his mouth and a heavy, bluish swelling was rising fast along his left cheek bone.

"All right, Shep," Brokaw murmured. "Right here."

Shep lifted burning eyes to him. After a moment he shook his head and swung away, murmuring: "It ain't because I want it. But the sheriff said we was to quit. I'll see you again." Retrieving his hat and fallen gun, he moved toward his horse.

The sheriff's satisfied, drawling voice said: "What's been goin' on here? You, Carl, what was this all about?"

The homesteader laid down his rifle and climbed onto the wagon. He took his wife in his arms, awkwardly trying to comfort her. Her crying had dissolved into muffled sobs as she tried, futilely, to cover her shoulders where Shep had ripped her dress away.

The cowpuncher addressed as Carl said: "Nothin' much, Ben. We caught this sodbuster on Arrowhead range. We was just teachin' him a lesson."

Brokaw whistled to the bay gelding and he trotted up. He knocked the dust from his hat, picked up his gun, and swung to the saddle, glancing again at Shep who now stood near his two companions.

The sheriff considered that information for a moment. Then he shifted his pale eyes to the homesteader. "What's ailin' your woman, mister?"

The man ducked his head at Shep. "That cowboy tried to force her into the back of the wagon while his friends here held me down with ropes." His voice began to tremble with anger. "Would have done it, too, if that fellow on the bay hadn't come along!"

All the friendliness vanished from the sheriff's voice. His face went flint hard. "That so, Shep?"

47

The cowboy made no reply, rubbing at the side of his face, his gaze on the ground.

The lawman drifted in closer to him. "I want an answer to that, Shep. How about it . . . you try that?"

Carl spoke up. "Shep wasn't meanin' no harm, Ben. Had hisself a couple of snorts out of a bottle and I reckon he sort of lost his head, seein' that woman."

"And you and Domino was just standin' by lettin' him do it," the sheriff observed with withering scorn. "That don't go in my county. You know that, Shep. All of you do. Any woman's safe around here."

"Safe!" the homesteader's wife echoed, finding her voice. "Nobody's safe in this god-forsaken country!" Suddenly she began to beat on her husband's chest in a wild, hopeless way. "I want to go home! I want to get out of this terrible country! I want to go back where people are civilized human beings, and not drunken beasts and murderers and thieves!"

Brokaw watched in silence. Shep and his two friends stirred restlessly, shame-faced and ill at ease. A woman's safety on the range was a thing taken for granted, but there were always exceptions and this was one of those. The homesteader comforted his wife, patting her heaving shoulders, stroking her straw-colored hair. He was a young man, not much older than Brokaw. His wife was a mere child.

The sheriff said: "I'd like for you folks to drive into town. You prefer charges against these men and I'll see they get taken care of."

The homesteader looked up. "That'd mean days and I ain't plannin' to spend any more time around here than I just have to. All I want is for people to let us alone long enough for us to get out of this country. I had my fill of it . . . it's too hard. Awful hard on a woman."

The sheriff shrugged his thin shoulders. "Just as you say. But a man finds it a hard row to hoe when people won't help him keep the law. Ain't nothin' I can do if you won't make a complaint." He swiveled his sharp gaze to Shep. "I'll be tellin' Preston about this."

Shep stirred. "Go ahead. Tell him. They was on Arrowhead grass and you know he don't like that."

"We were just crossing," the homesteader cut in. "I never stopped on it."

"Makes no difference," Shep said doggedly. "Arrowhead range is closed."

Frank Brokaw smiled grimly to himself at the turn of his luck. Preston. Shep and the other two men worked for him and Preston was the man he was looking for — and hoped to get a job with long enough to make certain inquiries. Now there would be the additional problem of Shep and maybe the others as well.

The homesteader pushed his wife gently into the depths of the wagon. He settled himself on the seat and picked up the reins. "How long before we'll be off this Arrowhead land?"

"Couple, three hours at least," the sheriff replied.

"It can't be too soon," the homesteader murmured. "And it'll be the last time anybody'll ever see us around here," he added sourly, clucking his team into motion.

"What about Indians?" the sheriff reminded him. "You will be gettin' into Indian country another day or so. Better lay over somewhere until you can join up with a train goin' east."

"I never saw none comin' out and I don't figure to see none goin' back," the man retorted. "Anyway, don't reckon they'd be no worse than men like these."

"Don't bet on it," the sheriff commented dryly and turned his back to the departing wagon.

"Move on now," he said to Shep and his friends. "If I ever hear of you, any of you, botherin' a woman again in my county, I won't wait for this fancy law we now got in this territory. I'll just take matters in my own hands like I used to do. You all hear that?"

They started off at once, pointing their horses due west. Brokaw waited, feeling the push of the old lawman's gaze on him. Now it would come, the usual careful probing. "You a pilgrim, too?"

Brokaw shrugged. "Possible." He had nothing against lawmen. His own father had been one and he had been proud of that fact. But experience in the last years had taught him it was wise to talk little in their presence and depend not at all upon their help. Naturally none of them took kindly to a stranger in their midst looking to kill one of their townsmen.

"Headin' which way?"

Brokaw waited out a long moment. "Is there a law in this country saying I've got to go a certain direction?"

The sheriff clucked softly. "You're mighty proddy, son," he observed with no show of heat. "Happens you're on closed range, and, if you ended up dead, I might try to notify your relations or friends, assumin' you got some. You're a stranger around here."

Brokaw nodded. "That's right."

"Well, it ain't healthy range for a stranger to get caught on. Hugh Preston don't take kindly to trespassin'. You just saw a sample of that."

"Big country," Brokaw replied laconically. "A man's got to cross it somewhere. Anyway, maybe I've come looking to see this Hugh Preston."

The sheriff surveyed him thoughtfully. "Well, you're the kind, all right."

"Meaning what?"

"Meanin' Hugh likes proddy riders. Like Shep and them two with him. Carl Willet and Domino."

Brokaw considered that in silence, not liking the comparison. But Preston was the man he was seeking and nothing must be permitted to stand in the way. Not after all the months of searching. To hell with Shep and the others. And the sheriff, too.

He said: "Preston's place to the south? There where the smoke is?"

The old lawman glanced over his shoulder. He ducked his head. "Fifteen miles or so. You goin' there now?"

Brokaw said — "Yes." — and wheeled the bay around. The sheriff swung the gray in next to him.

"Mind if I side along? When a man gets old, he finds lonesomeness a little hard to take. Kind of like he figured there wasn't much time left for talkin' and such, and he don't want to waste any."

Brokaw nodded. He would prefer to ride alone, in the silence he had come to appreciate as a trustworthy friend in the long hours of the days and nights. Perhaps he might learn something of value from the old lawman. But he would have to be careful with his own words; he could not afford to create any suspicion other than that any drifter would normally give rise to. And he must use care not to tip his hand.

"I'm Ben Marr, sheriff of this county. Don't think I heard you mention your name."

"No," Brokaw drawled, "you didn't."

Marr waited for him to continue. When, after a time, he did not, he said: "Find this country to your likin'?"

"I've seen better."

"Where?"

Brokaw swung his face to the lawman, grinning at the crudeness of the snare. "Several places."

Marr's bland expression did not change. "You know Hugh Preston?"

"Heard of him."

"Never worked for him before?"

"Like I said, I just heard of him. Never saw him, never worked for him."

"He send for you?"

Brokaw shook his head patiently. "No. Why?"

Marr wagged his grizzled head. "You don't know, then they's no use tellin' you. You figurin' to work for him?"

"Is he hiring hands?" Brokaw asked in a careful way.

"Roundup's gettin' close. Places like Preston's are always needin' 'punchers this time of year. Reckon you could hire on at any of the other spreads, too."

Brokaw made no reply to that suggestion. They rode silently on for the next two miles, the bay a half step behind the lawman's gray. Where the faint trail split, one bearing on toward the distant smudge of Preston's Arrowhead Ranch, the other to the town of Westport Crossing, Ben Marr pulled up. He screwed about in his saddle until he faced Brokaw squarely.

"If you'll take an old man's advice, son, you'll keep on ridin'. They's a lot of new country you can see outside this Scattered Hills range. I don't like to see a young feller get himself mixed up in things like goes on at Preston's."

For a swift moment Frank Brokaw had a fleeting remembrance of his father, of the kindness, the care and solicitation the man had always had for him. Ben Marr, in that fraction of time, was very much like Tom Brokaw. But it was because of Tom Brokaw, and the terrible thing done to him that he was here now, in the Scattered Hills, looking for Hugh Preston.

He gave the lawman a half smile. "Thanks, Sheriff. I can wipe my own nose. Don't lose any sleep over me."

Marr's shoulders lifted and fell in a sign of weary resignation. "All right. Only thing, someday trouble's goin' to pop like all get out there at Arrowhead. I'm hopin' I won't find you bogged down hock-deep in it."

The hard, tough shell that had momentarily vanished from Frank Brokaw suddenly was about him again, wrapping him with its bitter, cynical shield. "I'll be real careful, Sheriff," he replied in a faintly mocking tone, and swung off down the trail.

CHAPTER
THREE

Hugh Preston's Arrowhead Ranch was no ordinary, run-of-the-mill spread. This was apparent to Brokaw when he topped the last low rise and looked down upon the large, rambling structure with its outward scattering of smaller buildings. The main house was a long stone-and-log affair with a steeply slanted roof and shining white trim. Rugged, austere, and brutish, it reflected the great power it represented in a solid, foursquare sort of stance — defying man and the elements with its thick walls. It sat well to the fore in a broad clearing with several sheds, two barns, a cook shack, foreman's quarters, and a sprawling bunkhouse ranging out behind it to a grove of medium-aged trees on the west side.

Brokaw's studied gaze probed the place for a full five minutes while he memorized the grounds and the complete lay of the buildings. And, too, he was having some dark thoughts about the man who owned it. A lot of money had gone into building it, into stocking it with cattle — how much? He had his own ideas of the amount and that thought stirred him into action. He clucked the bay forward, going down the long slope.

Unconsciously he pulled the heavy gun at his hip around to a handier position. He had forced himself to learn the use of a handgun. He had never really grown accustomed to having it at his side. He preferred the strength of his arms and hands in a fight, and, if that was not the way it was to be, he liked the rifle now tucked in the boot beneath his leg. But a man couldn't always go walking around with a rifle slung in his arms.

No one was in sight when he approached, which was normal enough. Riders would be on the range working; the night crew would be getting some sleep in the bunkhouse. He reached the wide, hard-packed yard, and pointed for the tie rail at the front of the main house. There was a side door, also, leading into the forward rooms, but he chose the one he thought most apt to open into Preston's office. He had just reached the rail when a figure came into the open from the small building near the bunkhouse. The foreman, Brokaw guessed.

He halted, staying in the saddle, and waited for the man to come up. He was not a young man, somewhere in his early fifties. He wore the usual range work clothes, but he carried himself erect and with a strong show of authority, as though proud of what he was doing. An ancient, worn cedar-handled gun sagged at his hip, and, as he drew closer, Brokaw had a better look at his craggy, pointed features. His eyes were small, a piercing blue and deeply set. His face was dark from summer's sun and winter's bitter wind and deeply grooved, only partly hidden by a mustache that exactly matched his gray hair. His gaze was cool and level, showing neither friendliness nor enmity.

"You're a far piece from the main trail, cowboy."

Brokaw considered the hard, dry press of the man's voice, wondering if he might be Preston; too old, he finally concluded. They had said Preston was younger. This man was the foreman, no doubt.

He said: "Doing any hiring?"

The old cowboy studied him briefly. "You don't look much like a workin' hand," he said bluntly. "But I reckon we could use some riders . . . the kind that can nurse a cow. That what you had in mind?"

"What else?"

Over in one of the barns a man was whistling tunelessly and somewhere a horse nickered, getting wind of the bay and recognizing a newcomer. A cricket clacked in the dry grass along Preston's house, and, high above the Sierra Diablos, much closer now, an eagle swooped in a lazy, circling pattern.

"Like I said, you don't look the kind."

"Well, what do I look like, then?" Brokaw asked in a soft voice.

The old cowpuncher shrugged. "You didn't get them big arms and that pair of shoulders singin' lullabies to a night herd. But never mind. Always need hands this time of the year and a man can't afford his choosin's. Forty dollars and chuck. You want it, go over to the bunkhouse and find yourself a bed. What's your handle?"

"Brokaw. Frank Brokaw."

The man thought hard for a moment. "Name's not familiar," he said then. "I'm Abel Cameron, foreman for Mister Preston." He paused, as the side door swung in and a tall, spare man came from the main house into the sunlight. "That's him, there," he finished.

Brokaw swiveled his attention to the cattleman, the hair along the back of his neck suddenly stiffening. Here now was Hugh Preston; here was the man he had heard about in Tascosa. Here, by all probabilities, was Matt Slade.

He was a good-looking man. He approached in the short, mincing steps of a man unused to walking and disliking every step of it. He had a squared sort of carriage and good shoulders, but the face failed to fit the body. It was finely cut, almost feminine, and his mouth had a weakness about the corners. His eyes were dark on either side of a thin nose and his hair, bared to the sun, was a washed-out blond. Brokaw met his glance with a steady gaze.

"Who's this, Abel?"

"Man I just hired on. Name of Frank Brokaw."

Long ago Brokaw had stopped giving a false name. At first it seemed a smart idea when he made his inquiries, but later he decided it was far better to come right out with it — to make himself known. It would serve to bring matters to a quick head once he met the man who was Matt Slade. He closely watched Preston's eyes, his reactions, searching for any signs of alarm or wariness. Preston surveyed him curiously for a moment.

He said: "Good. Could use a half dozen more. Cattle's scattered pretty wide, Abel. We got to get them all in this year." He came back to Brokaw. "You new in this country, Frank?"

"First time around," Brokaw replied.

Preston smiled, showing even, small teeth that were gleaming white. "Glad to have you on the crew. Take your orders from Abel here, and mind your own business and you'll make out all right."

He wheeled away, striking for the cook shack with its narrow dining quarters attached. Brokaw watched him leave with half-shut eyes, having his suspicions about the man. He was a smooth one and cool as they came. He was the right build and about the described age.

Cameron broke into his thoughts. "One thing about Mister Preston, either he likes a man, or he sure don't. They's no middle ground with him. I reckon he likes you."

Brokaw swung down from the gelding. "I wonder why," he murmured.

Cameron threw a hasty, sharp glance at him. "You think he's got a special reason?"

"He's your friend, you ought to know," Brokaw replied in an easy tone. "My horse has been traveling for quite a spell. I reckon I better draw me another from the corral for the rest of the day. That all right?"

He felt the push of Cameron's blue eyes. The foreman was still trying to fathom his words, read some meaning into them. But he said no more about it. "Sure. Either put him in the corral with the rest of the stock, or take him in the barn. Plenty of horses around here to draw from. You et yet?"

"Not since early this morning."

"Cookie'll have some grub ready before long. Not much sense in you goin' out on the range this late anyway. Just lay around the rest of the day and figure on ridin' in the mornin'. I'll toll you off to the boys tonight at supper."

Brokaw nodded, and led the bay off to the barn. He stabled him, pulled off the gear, and rubbed him down with a gunny sack, afterward pulling down some feed for him. Taking his saddlebags and blanket roll, he strolled through the dim recesses of the barn, throwing his search along the walls until he came at last to the tack room. This would be as good a time as any to look the gear over. There was no one in sight and he spent a full fifteen minutes going over the rack of hulls. Some were fairly new, some old, and there was one that had been completely shattered by a bullet that had struck the swell, but there was no silver-mounted saddle in the lot. Matt Slade had owned such a saddle when he had left Central City. The blaze-faced sorrel they said he rode likely had been sold, or maybe was dead, but the saddle was something else. Something a man usually hung onto after all else was gone. And its being a fancy, hand-tooled, silver-decorated job would make the attachment even stronger. Such a piece of gear Matt Slade probably would keep.

Or would he? If he was a smart man wanting to sever all connections to the past, he might also rid himself of that. Such saddles were not common, but it would not be said they were a rarity, either. Brokaw had seen a few down in Texas and in New Mexico, and some real fancy ones in California. But there was not one there in Arrowhead's tack room, and, if Hugh Preston was actually Matt Slade, he had played it real cozy and had gotten rid of the saddle, or else had it hidden away somewhere else. Possibly in the main house.

He left the barn's huge bulk and tramped across the yard to the bunkhouse. It was a large, rectangular affair with double tiers of bunks running along either side and two tables with chairs down the center. Moving softly so as to not awaken the half dozen or more snoring men, he found a bunk that appeared to be unused and, throwing his blanket and bags onto the thin pad, sat down, his thoughts still on Hugh Preston.

The rancher could easily be Matt Slade. He fitted the meager description obtained back in Central City. And he was a smart man, you could see that. One easily capable of controlling his feelings if the name Brokaw had had any special meaning to him. But he had to be sure, he recognized that fact; he had to find more proof, something definite before he broached Preston, bald-faced, with his suspicions.

Thinking of this, he stretched out on his bunk. He fell asleep, passing up the noon meal, and came awake late in the day to the thud of riders pulling into the yard. Rousing himself, he went outside into the falling dusk, nodding to the curious glances of the men he encountered. He cleaned up at the wash house in the rear of the crew's quarters, and, when the supper iron clanged its summons across the graying day, he crossed over to the cook shack and entered.

Abel Cameron was there ahead of him and pointed a gnarled finger to a place on his left at the plank table. Other riders began streaming in as the cook, a squat, dark-faced Mexican, started bringing platters of steak, potatoes, hominy and boiled cabbage. Two large coffee pots were stationed on the table, one at either end. The cowpunchers fell to at once, talking little as they ate. Preston was not there and Brokaw recognized only three men other than the foreman: the man he had tangled with, Shep, and his two companions, Carl and Domino. Twice he glanced up to find Shep's eyes boring him in a hard, angry way.

When the platters were empty and the final cup of coffee poured, Cameron got to his feet.

"Boys, this here," he said, waving his hand at Brokaw, "is a new man hired on today. Name of Frank Brokaw." He paused, as attention swung around and came to a stop on Brokaw. "He's a Johnny-come-lately to this part of the country so I don't reckon he knows nobody here." He hesitated again, turning now to Brokaw. "Frank, this ain't all the Arrowhead crew, but it'll do as a start. First man here on my right is Jack Corbett."

Corbett, a freckle-faced redhead acknowledged the introduction with a nod, reserving, as was customary, any further overtures until he became better acquainted.

"Next one," Cameron continued, "is Buckshot Martin. Then Pete Sampson. Then Jules Strove and Carl Willet. Only name next feller's got is Domino.

61

Never heard him mention no other 'un, so I reckon that's all of it." Cameron halted, eyeing the next cowpuncher closely. "What happened to you, Shep? Fall offen your horse and skin up a mite? Or did one them brush-lovin' longhorns take a fancy to you? That feller is Shep Russell, Brokaw."

The old foreman droned on, introducing three more men, the last a powerfully built, handsome cowboy with a neatly trimmed mustache. He was Ollie Godfrey, Cameron said, and he eyed Brokaw with a steady intentness.

The room was quiet after that, as if the final introduction had some deeper, more important meaning. Godfrey ran his fingers through his wavy blond hair. He nodded and in a lazy voice said: "I see grampa has made you right at home."

Brokaw said nothing, suddenly fully aware of a sullen undercurrent in the room. One of the riders chuckled. Shep Russell. He was appreciating Godfrey's small joke and in so doing was letting Brokaw know upon which side he stood. Cameron's face had gone stiff and his eyes were glinting, steel-blue points.

He said: "There's always a cute one in every outfit, Frank. I reckon Ollie's our boy."

Godfrey made no reply in the ensuing silence. Brokaw recognized then the bad blood that existed between the two and had a brief wonder at its cause. But he gave it little thought, having his own immediate problems concerning Hugh Preston. Two of the riders pushed back from the table, and an immediate exodus of the others began.

Cameron turned to Brokaw. "We start early around here. Breakfast at four-thirty sharp."

Brokaw nodded. His glance was upon Shep Russell. That man had not stirred, but was watching him with a hot, burning gaze. He was not forgetting the affair earlier in the day, where the homesteader was concerned, and it was plain he meant to do something about it.

Brokaw moved by Cameron, his face suddenly dark and still. He well knew Shep Russell's kind — they understood but one thing — toughness and brute strength. He walked to where the cowboy sat, fingers laced across his belly, leaning back in his chair. Lifting his foot, he gave the chair a hard shove. Russell went over backward in a crashing heap.

Cameron yelled something in his surprise. Godfrey and the cowboy called Jules Strove, and Carl Willet, the only riders still in the room, stepped quickly away from Russell's thrashing shape. Russell got to his feet, his face working with fury, curses streaming from his lips.

"Damn you! I'll kill you for that! I'll . . ."

"You act like a man with something on your mind," Brokaw said in a winter-cold voice. "I'm ready to hear it."

Russell's mouth ceased its working. He stared at Brokaw's threatening figure for a long moment. Then: "When I'm ready. I'll pick the place."

"This place is good as any."

A wild temper was racing through Russell, leaving him uncertain and at a loss as to his own abilities. He seemed half inclined to reach for the gun at his hip but something, some deep and wiser caution, was holding him back. Perhaps it was the absolute calm, the utter deadliness of Brokaw, or possibly the flatness of his eyes. His gaze broke suddenly and he looked away, glaring angrily at the other men in the room — at the Mexican cook who had entered at the crash of the overturning chair. With a hurried motion, he wheeled away and bolted for the doorway.

Brokaw threw out a broad, hindering hand against Russell's shoulder. He pushed, and Russell fell back a step. In a cold voice Brokaw said: "All right, Shep. I'll let it pass for this time. But keep out of my way. Understand?"

Russell gave him a furious, frustrated look. Nodding, he rushed for the door, slammed through it, and went lunging out into the yard.

Brokaw remained still, letting the tension run from his tall figure. His back was to Cameron and to the others, and there was only the sound of their breathing in the room. Finally Cameron spoke, his voice plaintive.

"Didn't know you and Shep had met up before."

"Just once," Brokaw replied.

The old foreman's face hardened. "I ain't knowin' what's between you two but I want no trouble around here. If you're the trouble-makin' kind, just move along. I got me enough problems without that."

"There'll be no trouble as long as he stays out of my way. But get this straight, Cameron, I'm of no mind to put up with his foolishness."

Cameron stroked his mustache. "Fair enough. I reckon Shep understands that, too. What's between the two of you, anyway?"

"Matter for us, nobody else."

Cameron's ire lifted again. "Long as you both are workin' for Arrowhead, I say it's my business, me bein' foreman of this crew."

"Then you better ask Shep about it."

"Maybe I will," Cameron said. "Howsomever, I reckon this spread's big enough for both of you. See you in the mornin'."

He moved to the doorway and out into the yard. Jules Strove and Willet followed, but Ollie Godfrey hung back. He walked up beside Brokaw. His face was cold and his eyes were hard.

"You'd be a smart man to move on, drifter. There's no job around here for you, leastwise a healthy one."

Brokaw favored him with a down-curling grin. "Second time today I've been told that. Fact is, I like it here."

"You may not like it so good later," Godfrey said. "And don't be pinning your bets on old man Cameron. He won't be ram-rodding this outfit much longer."

Brokaw said nothing. So that was the trouble between Cameron and Godfrey. The husky cowboy was gunning for the old foreman's job. He found himself not liking the blond man, not only because of his cocksure, belligerent manner, but for some other reason he could not quite pin down.

"Is this Hugh Preston's idea?"

Godfrey said: "No business of yours that I can see. But it'll happen. You can figure on it."

"So?"

"Take that advice you got and move on. There'll be no job here on Arrowhead for you."

Godfrey turned abruptly to the doorway and walked into the yard. Brokaw stood quietly by the long table for another minute or two, his eyes lost in the dusk outside the room. Then his wide shoulders moved in a gesture of indifference. Hell with Godfrey and Abel Cameron. That was their own fight. He had Matt Slade to find and kill.

CHAPTER
FOUR

Brokaw came out into the wide yard and strolled toward the pole corrals. It was not yet entirely dark but night's curtain was rising swiftly, and some of the lamps were already lit. Sounds, emanating from a noisy game of stud poker in the bunkhouse, broke the evening's hush at intervals, mingling with an occasional thud in the barn where part of the horses fed and rested.

He came to a stop at the wagon shed. Placing his shoulders against its wall, he drew the makings from a pocket and spun up a cigarette. A match flared, orange and bright under his thumbnail, and, as he held it close, its flame mirrored against the hard polished planes of his face and gave his eyes a splintery look. Not all of the temper was out of his long frame yet, but he felt better. Shep Russell would stay out of his way for a long time, at least.

He sucked in a deep draft of smoke, tipped back his head, and blew it out in a single, trailing cloud. The spring night was soft about him, only a bit chilly and sweet with the smells of summer coming to life. Once begun, darkness moved in quickly, and the shadows became deep voids of black. Cameron came from his quarters and rapped across the hard pack to the ranch house. He thumped on the door and, to the muffled response, opened it and entered.

Two men came then from the bunkhouse, walking slowly, at ease, their cigarettes small red eyes in the obscurity. They passed under the bunkhouse window's square of light, and Brokaw recognized one as Jules Strove, the other as the redhead, Jack Corbett. Strove was chuckling.

"Man and boy. You should 'a' seen old Shep's face when that feller Brokaw knocked over his chair. He looked like a ranny what had just backed into a hot brandin' iron."

"And Shep didn't take him up on it?" Corbett noted in a wondering tone.

"Uhn-uh. Not Shep, not any of Ollie's bunch. He just stood there quiet as a fly walkin' on fresh butter, and listened while Brokaw told him what's what. Then he skedaddled. Went out the door like a cow critter that had just seen a she-bear with cubs."

"Can't say as I blame him," the redhead mused. "Something about that Brokaw that makes a man think twice before he ups and starts fiddlin' with him."

The men passed on by, enjoying their final smokes before turning in. Brokaw grinned into the darkness. That was the way he wanted it, that was just how he wanted them to feel. Maybe they would all mind their own business and leave him to his. The sooner he got to the bottom of Hugh Preston's past life, the sooner he could wind up his affairs and get out of the country.

Ranch life and work no longer appealed to him. It was hard, back-breaking labor in all sorts of weather, and for little pay. He could think off-hand of a dozen better ways to make a living, all of them offering better money. There was a greater depth of danger involved, of course, but a man didn't mind that. It just added zest to the job and somewhere down the last few years that had become a strong necessity, it seemed.

It had not always been that way. He guessed it was the war that brought about the change. Before that he had not minded it, possibly because he knew nothing else other than working the small farm-ranch his father owned. With only a couple of men and his mother, he had operated the place while his father carried on with his job as marshal. Then the war fever had seeped into his blood.

He remembered the look on his father's face that evening, when he had suddenly announced at the supper table that he was going to enlist. Tom Brokaw, a cup of coffee halfway to his lips, paused, looked keenly at him, and then carefully replaced the cup in its saucer.

"I reckon if that's what you want, boy, that's what you'll have. I ain't standing in your way. But if you go, I want you to be a soldier, not one of them thieving, raiding, killing for the devil of it cut-throats. A man needs a reason to shoot another man, and, if you are believing in this cause, then you got a right to fight for it. And when you come back, winner or loser, you can come back proud of what you've done, and not be afraid somebody'll remember you for something bad."

It was the longest speech he had ever heard his father make at one time, and he never forgot it. His mother, who he recalled as a tired, work-worn woman, had cried softly at first when it came time for him to leave. But she squared her slight shoulders, kissed him on the cheek, and pressed a small Bible into his hands.

"You get sick, Son, you come home," she had admonished him. She had never fully conceded he was no longer her small boy. "And when the war is over, you come straight home."

But he had not. He was just twenty-one when Lee laid down the sword, a boy turned overly fast into a man by war's harsh and bloody realities. He was sick of fighting, of killing, of hiding, of rain, mud, heat, cold, and the smell of cordite and the sight of a gun repulsed him. A terrible restlessness had possessed him, and he gave way to its demands.

Finally he returned to Kansas, the scars only partly healed, to face a world of cold, half friends and total strangers.

John Tennyson, the banker had said: "Figured you'd turn up someday. We tried to find you but nobody knew what happened to you. Some said you were dead. Two, three letters we sent came back."

"What happened? What happened to my folks?"

"Well, this man Matt Slade was a friend of your pa's. Showed up here one day, just passing through, he said. But he hadn't seen your pa for a long spell, so he stuck around, just visiting. Guess he was around here for three weeks or better. Used to see him walking and riding with your pa. Reckon he stayed there at the place with them, too."

"Where did he come from?"

"Don't rightly know. Reckon I never did hear him or your pa say. Anyway, along about that time I had a shipment of gold coin come in. Nearly ten thousand dollars. It was to be picked up by a land syndicate that was planning to buy up a lot of ground around here. Nobody knew about that money except your pa and me, and maybe the stage driver."

"You trying to tell me pa had something to do with stealing that money?"

"I'm coming to that. Matt Slade found out about the gold somehow, and the only place I figure it could have come from was your pa, because I sure never mentioned it. Then one morning, about four o'clock, we woke up to a big explosion. Everybody went tearing down to find out what it was and I spotted the smoke coming out of my bank. So did the others and we all got there about the same time. We saw this man Slade leaving on his horse, but he had caught us flat-footed and there wasn't nobody saddled up to chase him. There was a little shooting and some say he was hit, but we never did know for sure."

"And pa . . . what about him?"

"We found him laying there in the bank with his head all caved in. Looked like he had been standing across the room from the vault, and, when the explosion came, a piece of the door flew over and hit him. Poor Tom. It'd been better if it had killed him. He didn't know anything. His mind was a blank and it never changed."

"But there was no proof he had been in on it with Slade."

"Then what was he doing in there with him?"

"He maybe suspected Slade was up to something and followed him there. He might have stepped into the room just as the charge went off. You sure don't think he had anything to do with it, do you?"

Tennyson had wagged his head. "I only know what we all saw, and the general opinion around was that Slade and Tom were in it together. Ten thousand dollars is a lot of money. Thinking about it can do things to a man."

"But not to my pa. There's not enough gold in this world to make him do something like that."

Frank Brokaw had been shocked, bewildered, and angered, and for several minutes he had vented his feelings in the small confines of the Central City Bank. But after a time a measure of calmness had come back to him.

"What did you do to him, after you'd decided what you did?"

Tennyson shrugged. "No point in doing anything to him. His mind was gone, like I said. He stayed out on the farm with your mother. Then that winter she took down and died. There wasn't anything left to do but send him to Leavenworth where they could take care of him."

The calloused words had ripped through Frank Brokaw, a bitter, steel-hard determination had swirled within him and crystallized into an inflexible core. He had said: "Nobody ever heard of Matt Slade again?"

"Nobody. Podie Wilkins did a lot of looking around the country, and the land syndicate sent out an Eastern detective, but they didn't turn up anything. He just dropped out of sight."

"I'll find him," Brokaw had murmured. "I'll find him and bring him back here, and make him admit Pa had nothing to do with the robbing of your bank. And then I'll kill him, because that's what he did to them. Killed them both, sure as I'm standing here."

"Hardly any use . . . ," Tennyson had begun, but Brokaw had cut him short.

"What did this Matt Slade look like?"

"Big man, nigh as tall as you. Good-looking but I just don't recollect anything special about his face. He'd be about forty now, I'd guess. Rode a big, blaze-faced sorrel stallion and sported a silver-mounted saddle. Had silver coins fastened all along the edge of the skirt."

"You sure Slade was his real name?"

"Only thing I ever heard, and that's what your pa called him . . . Matt Slade."

It wasn't much to go on, but Frank Brokaw had filed each detail carefully in his mind, adding to it a few other bits garnered from different townspeople. Podie Wilkins had turned over to him his father's gun and belt, and he had brushed aside the blood-washed memories of the war, and strapped it on. He had spent hours practicing a fast draw, and, when he felt he could hold his own in that department, he had turned to improving his accuracy. But he had spent little time on that; when he found Matt Slade, he would be standing close enough that he could not miss.

And so it began. The search for the man who had called himself Matt Slade. At the outset he knew that would not be his name now. He would have changed that just as he would have taken great pains to slash all other connections to the past. But a man with $10,000 gold to spend could not very well hide his glittering light under a bushel. Not in the West anyway, where such things did not escape notice.

John Tennyson and Podie Wilkins and many others had told him flatly he was undertaking a hopeless task, that he should forget it, move back on the farm, get it going, and then bring his father to live out the remainder of his days with him. But that was not the way of Frank Brokaw. He would find Matt Slade, drag a confession from him that Tom Brokaw was innocent of any wrongdoing — then kill him.

In the months that followed he had met a few people who recalled the big red stallion and the fancy saddle, none who remembered the man who rode them. But he did eventually find several who recalled a big man who appeared in the Scattered Hills country around five years back, a man who came from nowhere, who paid cash for the old Cresswell place, and who rebuilt it with an extravagant hand, sparing no cost. That man was Hugh Preston.

Brokaw came back to the present as a curse exploded from the bunkhouse. There was a burst of laughter. A door banged and one of the riders, Buckshot Martin it seemed to Brokaw yet standing there in the dark, came out and stomped for the wash house. Brokaw heard him stroking the hand pump as he drew for himself a

74

drink of water. Two more came out, Ollie Godfrey and Shep Russell. They drifted into the center of the yard, well away from the crew's quarters.

"How much longer you figure?" Shep was saying as they came within earshot.

Godfrey puffed at his half-burned cigar. "Not much. She's due back in a few days now."

"You're mighty sure of her."

Godfrey laughed. "I am. She's in the palm of my hand, don't you forget it."

The side door of the main house swung back and Cameron came into view. Shep Russell moved off toward the wash house, and Godfrey, hooking his thumbs into his belt, swung fully around and watched the foreman approach. Faint star shine flooded the yard, turning all things pale and blurred and deepening the shadowed areas. The Mexican cook's handful of chickens, in their makeshift pen behind the kitchen, chattered sleepily as something disturbed them.

Ollie Godfrey called across the hard pack: "Well, grampa, you get your night's kissin' done?"

Cameron broke his stride and came to a slow halt.

Godfrey's voice, pushing, sarcastic, deliberately pitched to irritate, said: "Not much use in your doing it, old man. You're through. No amount of talking is going to keep you on this job, and the sooner you make up your mind to that, the better off we'll all be."

"I could do a little talkin' on my own, Ollie," Cameron said coolly. "A few things Mister Preston wouldn't much like hearin'."

Godfrey laughed again, in a soft, taunting way. "But you won't, grampa. You'd be a dead man. It would be like committing suicide and that you full well know."

"Maybe so," Cameron murmured. "Maybe so. Seems to me you're crowdin' things right fast lately. What's eatin' at you?"

"Something you'd not understand, old man. Only thing, don't be making any plans for the future. Leastwise, not as foreman for this outfit."

Abel Cameron thought for a minute. Then: "So that's it. Well, I was foreman when Cresswell had this place and I've been the same ever since Hugh Preston took it over. Reckon I'll keep on being same until he tells me different."

Cameron paused. Brokaw could see his jutting profile pointing straight at Godfrey, hostility in every angle of his craggy face. "Place like this takes a man, not a slick-ear at the head."

There was a breathless pause, and then Godfrey started forward. "Maybe I better show you what a man is . . . ," he said.

Cameron waited, motionless. Brokaw moved out from the shadows along the wagon shed. He came into the faint shine near the middle of the distance separating the two men. Cameron glanced quickly to him and Ollie Godfrey pulled to a sudden stop. His face came around, angry and surprised.

"What's this . . . ?" he began.

Brokaw, his eyes reaching out beyond the two men, located Shep Russell over by the bunkhouse and gave his dim shape a momentary survey. He waved his hand, indicating the cigarette between his fingers. "Just having a smoke," he said calmly. "However, you do flap your mouth a little wide."

Abel Cameron chuckled. Godfrey's face went stiff. He flung a hasty glance over his shoulder, saw no one, and came back to Brokaw's languorous shape. "You're horning in where you got no business," he said in a low voice. "Look out you don't go saddling the wrong horse."

"I'll take my chances," Brokaw replied softly.

"That's just what they'll be," Godfrey retorted, and pivoted on his heel for the bunkhouse.

Brokaw and Cameron watched him cross the hard pack and stamp into the crew's quarters. When the door had banged behind him, the foreman turned to Brokaw.

"Obliged to you, Frank. But they's no call for you to mix in this."

"I'm not," Brokaw said shortly. "Just happened to be standing around."

Cameron studied him for a moment. "I see. Well, all the same, I'm obliged to you."

He swung away, heading for his own bunk. All the lamps were out now. Preston's Arrowhead was quiet. Brokaw rolled another cigarette and cupped his hands over the match. Now there was Ollie Godfrey, he thought. He couldn't seem to stay clear of things. First it was Shep and maybe his two friends, Carl Willet and Domino. And, of course, Hugh Preston. If he had recognized Brokaw by name, he, too, like the others, would have things on his mind. Briefly he considered his position. A man might find it hard to sleep in a room where others were not exactly friendly.

He flipped the cigarette into the yard, watching its coal flare up brightly and die, then turned about. He moved by the wagon shed, circling it, coming out at the barn where he had stabled the bay. Entering the runway, he followed it out until he reached the ladder leading up to the loft. He climbed that, gaining the upper level, piled high with fragrant hay. There he bedded down for the night.

CHAPTER
FIVE

After breakfast in that chill, half light preceding dawn, Abel Cameron hailed the Arrowhead crew together. He issued his orders for the day, turning last to Frank Brokaw.

"You take the two-seater and head for town. Missus Preston's comin' in on the stage. Pick her up and bring her back."

At once Ollie Godfrey pushed forward, anger in his eyes. "Why him? None of us been to town in weeks. Why not let me go?"

Cameron said: "Reckon that's the reason. Everybody can't go, so I figure it wouldn't be fair to send any of you."

"Rest of the boys won't mind me going," Godfrey persisted.

"Brokaw'll make the trip," Cameron said, and wheeled away.

For a long minute Godfrey stared after the foreman's stiff figure, but after a time he shrugged and moved off toward the corral. Brokaw turned for the barn where the wrangler had the carriage, with its two fine blacks, already waiting for him. Cameron was there ahead of him. He said: "How'll I know Missus Preston?"

The old foreman gave him a brief grin. "You'll know her. Never you fret over that."

Brokaw climbed onto the cushioned seat and gathered up the ribbons. "How far to town and which road do I take?"

"You'll be all the mornin' gettin' there. Take the road to the right after you leave the yard. Stay on it all the way."

Brokaw nodded and swung the blacks into motion. They rolled out of the yard, but just as they drew parallel with the front of the ranch house, Brokaw caught movement from the corner of his eye. He flung a quick glance to that point. Hugh Preston was standing at the corner of the log structure, watching him with a studied, careful gaze. How long he had been there Brokaw had no way of knowing, but possibly for some minutes. It was too far, and the light was much too poor to see the rancher's features distinctly, but Brokaw had the feeling Preston's survey, hard and searching, had been upon him during the entire time he had been in the yard. The thought — *Preston is suspicious.* — sprang immediately into his mind. And that, logically, led to the conclusion that Preston and Matt Slade were one and the same, else why the suspicion?

He had a moment's urge to halt the blacks, wheel around, and throw his accusation into Preston's face. But a saner force moved in and thrust the impulse into the background of his mind. After all, what proof did he actually have? One or two circumstantial items, and now this close watch Preston had placed on him. You could hardly call that definite proof.

The blacks reached the crossroad and swung south into the deeper, sandier ruts. It was cool and they were in high spirits, so he let them have their kittenish way for the first few miles. When they had worked off their steam, he pulled them down to a comfortable trot and settled himself for the long ride.

He had not known Hugh Preston was married. He wondered if he had been so when he had called himself Matt Slade, if Slade he truly was. There had been no mention of a wife in Central City. But that was easy to explain. She would not have been with him, if he had come there with the predetermined intention of robbing a bank. More than likely, he had been a single man at that time, and it was after he had gotten his hands on the money that he took to himself a wife. There is nothing like a wife to suggest respectability.

Brokaw ran his glance idly over the landscape, sliding by at a steady gray-green pace. The bright sparkle of dew still held before the sun's lifting rays. But it would not be that way for long. In another hour or two the heat would move in, drying the tips of the grass, sucking off the juices, and changing the prairie to pale tan.

The country changed little with the miles. Only slightly more than flat, it stretched out in all directions, broken very occasionally by a lifting hill, a clump of cottonwoods, or a low, frowning butte. The Sierra Diablos stood aloof and deep blue in the background far to the west. Even at such distance they appeared rough and forbidding, as if trying to repudiate the undulatory, regular beauty of the prairies.

It was shortly after 11:00a.m. when he reached the edge of Westport Crossing and wheeled into its single main street. It had the same, general weather-worn appearance of all such towns, Brokaw observed. A twin row of high, false-fronted buildings, all badly in need of paint, standing shoulder to shoulder facing each other across a dusty, wide avenue. At that hour, few people were abroad and the narrow wooden sidewalks were nearly deserted.

He headed the blacks toward the far end of town, where a sign jutting out into the street proclaimed *Bell's Livery Stable*. The team was hot and a little tired from the steady run and he was himself bone-dry and hungry. He spotted the Longhorn Bar and made a mental note of its location.

A little farther on he singled out the Gem Café, looking clean and inviting behind panels of frothy white window curtains, and such information he filed along with the rest.

"Here! You there! Arrowhead!"

The voice of a woman came reaching out from the porch of the Westport Hotel. Brokaw swung his glance to that point, seeing at once the tall, striking shape of the speaker standing next to a pile of luggage. That would be Hugh Preston's wife. He pulled the team in, slanting for the porch, going over the woman carefully with half-shut eyes.

She was tall and well-formed in a suit of powder blue. Her honey-blonde hair was caught up and piled high under a perky straw hat, and, as he drew closer, he could see her eyes were blue, slightly almond-shaped, set in a triangular face. He hauled up the team in front of the porch and touched the brim of his hat.

"You're late, cowboy," she stated flatly. "Load these bags and let's get the hell out of here!"

Brokaw's glance flicked her briefly, then a faint humor touched the corners of his long mouth. He climbed from the carriage and stowed the luggage in the back seat. She did not wait for him to assist her, but was already in the seat when he was finished. He stepped into the vehicle, took up the reins, and continued on for the livery stable.

They traveled perhaps fifty feet before she became aware of it. She whirled on him. "Where do you think you're going?"

"Horses are tired. They need a little rest and feed."

"Forget the horses!" Darla Preston snapped. "Turn this rig around and get started for the ranch. I want to get home!"

"After the team feeds and waters," Brokaw replied calmly. "I'm a bit dry and hungry myself."

She reached suddenly across his arm and grasped the reins, jerking hard with all her strength. But Brokaw's hand was firm; the team scarcely felt the interference. With his free hand Brokaw pulled loose her fingers and pushed them away.

"Lady," he said then in an even tone, "you might just as well settle down. We're going nowhere until these horses, and I, have something to eat."

She was looking at him in an odd, startled way. Little flecks of anger danced in her eyes and her full lips were compressed into a stiff line. She said nothing. They reached Bell's, and Brokaw got out and handed her down from the seat, giving instructions for the care of the blacks to the hostler as he did so.

"Be pleased to have you eat dinner with me," he said as they moved back into the street.

"No thank you," she replied with a quick tilt of her head. She was almost as tall as he, Brokaw noticed. "Who are you anyway? What's your name? I don't remember seeing you around the ranch before."

"You haven't. Just started today. The name is Brokaw."

"Well, Brokaw, you haven't heard the last of this."

"Horses need attention. No sense in ruining a fine team like those blacks."

"Who cares about the horses? We've got plenty of them. Hereafter, when you're with me, you'll do what I tell you to. Understand that?"

The patience ran out of Frank Brokaw in one final drop. "Look," he said, "I'll be starting for the Arrowhead Ranch in one hour. You want to ride with me, you be standing over there on the porch of the hotel. If you don't want to wait, best thing you can do is start walking."

He wheeled about, leaving her standing there near the center of the street, and headed for the café. He did not bother to look back, and it was only after he had sat down and ordered his meal, that he glanced toward the hotel and saw her waiting on the porch. Women like

84

Darla Preston found small favor with him. He had no time to cater to their spoiled whims and notions. But she was a beautiful woman, he had to admit it. Exactly the sort you would expect Hugh Preston to marry, and she, in turn, was the kind that would go for a man with plenty of money.

His meal arrived: steak, potatoes, apple pie, and strong coffee. He ate unhurriedly, enjoying the food with the relish of a man sick of his own cooking. When he was finished, he paid the ticket and returned to the street. The sun was full high, bearing down hard, and he paused to brush the sweat from his brow with the back of a hand.

He turned sharply left, striking for the stables at the end of the street, the urgency to settle with Hugh Preston pushing him with relentless force. Thus he did not see Darla Preston standing just within the hotel's lobby where she had moved to escape the dust and heat, nor witness the look of puzzled interest on her face. He reached Bell's and entered. The hostler had seen him coming, and was leading the blacks to where the two-seater was parked, when he stepped into the shadowy runway. He helped the man finish the harnessing and a few minutes later drove to the hotel.

Darla was waiting on the porch. He helped her to the seat, settled down beside her, then they moved off down the street — with the brunt of a full noon heat bearing down upon them. The team had no inclinations to run now, as it had earlier in the day, but was content to trot along at a fair pace.

They drove in silence for the first five miles, Brokaw lost in his own thoughts, Darla a quiet, erect figure, smelling faintly of lilac, at his elbow. He turned to her then, recalling Ben Marr's face, and caught her staring at him. She pulled her glance away quickly.

"The sheriff asked to be remembered," he lied.

She murmured — "Oh." — in a way that said it meant little to her.

"He a friend of the family's?"

Darla laughed, a light, sparkling sound tinged at the edges by sarcasm. "Hardly. If he sent his regards, it was for some reason. Why?"

Brokaw shrugged and leaned forward, placing his elbows on his knees. "The way he talked, I figured him to be your friend."

"He's never approved of Hugh. Nor of me. I think he would like very much to get something bad on us. Natural, I suppose. The big ranchers are always targets."

"Has he been sheriff around here long?"

"Ever since we've been in this country. Little over six years."

Six years! Brokaw smiled his satisfaction. That much of the report was true; he had it now, not from hearsay but straight from Preston's wife. He began a question relative to their previous home, to that time before they had purchased Arrowhead, but she spoke before he voiced it.

"Why didn't Ollie come after me?"

"I was the only one not tied up."

Darla laughed again, having some secret joke about that. Brokaw recalled the young cowboy's obvious disappointment and resentment at not being allowed to make the trip. And he remembered the words spoken by him to Shep Russell the previous evening, wondering what, if any, connection they had.

The blacks trotted steadily onward. The carriage top cut off the strong thrust of the sun and rode easily over the rutted trail. Far ahead, to the right, a ballooning cloud of dust rode the hot air, drifting slowly toward them. Brokaw watched it with interest.

"You a friend of Hugh's?"

To her question Brokaw said: "No. Just came along looking for a job. Cameron hired me on."

She had forgotten apparently her anger of the morning and now seemed inclined to talk. "You don't look or act like the usual run of 'punchers."

"No? How does the usual 'puncher look and act?"

She did not immediately reply. He knew she was having difficulty in framing an answer. That he did not jump when she commanded, that he did not kowtow to her presence and stand in awe of her majestic imperiousness and beauty — those were her reasons, but she did not express them in so many words. She made a small, upflung gesture with her gloved hands. "Well, you just don't seem like it, that's all. You look more like . . ."

"Like a gunman," he supplied dryly.

"Yes," she stated flatly, and stopped short.

"Every man around here wears a gun. No call to peg me as a gunslinger because I hang one on my hip. The fact of the matter is, I hate them."

Brokaw again felt the pressure of her gaze, searching, wondering, prying deep. It came to him that she was trying to place him, catalog him, and, woman-like, place him somewhere in the proper niche in her mind. Possibly for future use.

She said: "Yes, it would be that way." Then, boldly and bluntly: "Where did you come from, Brokaw?"

He gave her a brief glance. "Around. Texas, Mexico, the territories. You name it, I've probably been there."

"In the war?"

"Four years of it."

"But I meant, where was your home? Where did you grow up?"

He accorded that question the silence it deserved, making no reply.

When she saw she had erred, she said: "Forget I asked that. I know certain men don't like to have their backgrounds gone into too deeply."

He had his own secret amusement at that, but made no comment. They dropped into a shallow valley that was like a broad soup bowl of grass, followed out the road that curved across its floor, and gained the opposite rim. Another basin dropped away ahead of them and they started the descent, coming suddenly upon a small herd of cattle being driven by a slim girl and a bearded old cowpuncher. The herd was about halfway past. Brokaw pulled the blacks to a slow walk.

"Drive on!" Darla Preston commanded, all at once tense and irritable.

The steers began to veer and mill at the appearance of the carriage, which had come so unexpectedly upon

88

them. Brokaw shook his head and hauled back on the reins, bringing the blacks to a stop.

"Drive through them!" Darla ordered in a terse voice. She leaned forward, grabbing for the whip.

Brokaw, his jaw set, jammed his booted foot against the whip's handle, wedging it in its socket. The slim girl, sitting straight in her saddle and watching them intently, wheeled and loped up.

"Damn you . . . damn you," Darla gritted through clenched teeth. "Why didn't you do what I told you!"

"Why?" Brokaw said, eyeing her closely. "Those people are having a hard enough time of it without making it worse. Had we butted into that drive, we likely would have got a horse horned, as well as splitting up their herd into a dozen bunches."

"I know that," Darla replied in a tight voice.

The girl on the horse stopped, her eyes sparking. "I had begun to wonder if I was going to have to put a bullet in one of your horses to make you wait."

"Too bad you didn't try," Darla said coolly.

"Cattle crossing a road takes the right of way," the girl shot back.

"Not necessarily."

"You mean not necessarily where Arrowhead is concerned. Arrowhead has its way regardless of all others."

The brand on the stock was a Double R, or R-Connected as it was sometimes called. Brokaw tried to recall if he had heard of it before, but it struck no responsive chord. He turned his attention to the girl. Young, scarcely twenty, he guessed, with dark hair and eyes, and a small nose across which a spray of freckles laid a faint track. She sat her saddle with an easy assurance and a sort of proud arrogance, as though defying the world and all those in it who would dare cross her. She had a will of her own, she would backtrack for no one, particularly Darla Preston, it seemed.

"Why, yes," Darla was saying in honey-sweet tones, "Arrowhead is big enough to do what it wants . . . when it wants to."

"Someday you may find out that it's a mistaken notion you have."

"I'm sure, my dear, it won't be where you and your brother are concerned."

The girl looked away, throwing her glance over the herd now beginning to thin out as it came toward the tail end. Even in her loose, shapeless range clothing of Levi's and too large a shirt, Brokaw saw she was well-built.

"I'll not wait any longer!" Darla announced.

The slim girl swung back to her swiftly, her dark eyes snapping. "You'll sit right where you are until the last steer is across. The last one!"

"Too much dust," Brokaw murmured, striving to keep things at peace. "No use eating dust."

For the first time the girl seemed to notice him. She looked him over carefully, her gaze sharp and thorough. "You're a new one," she stated finally.

Brokaw regarded her with expressionless features. A vague sort of admiration for her was stirring within him. She had a lot of spirit and all the great power of Arrowhead did not frighten her one whit. He wondered then who she was and what trouble lay between her and the Prestons.

A steer broke out of line and raced off, doubling back in the direction from which it had come. Instantly the girl was after it, handling her pony like a veteran, expertly heading the longhorn, turning it and starting it back with the others. When she came up again, her eyes were bright with excitement, and the color had risen in her tanned face.

The herd had crossed. To Darla the girl said: "You and your friend can go now." A look of mischief came into her eyes. "By the way, what happened to Ollie? This your new one?"

"Get this team moving, Brokaw," Darla breathed in a suppressed, furious way.

"The dust is still pretty thick."

"The hell with the dust! Get moving, I tell you!"

"You didn't answer my question, Darla dear," the girl called in a tantalizing voice.

Darla Preston wrenched the whip from its socket and swung it. It slashed through the air with a vicious whine, missing the girl by scant inches. Brokaw snatched it from her hand. He heard the slim girl laugh as she spun away.

"That little snip!" Darla fumed. "That cheap little beggar! She'll get her come-uppance! I'll see to that!"

Brokaw glanced at the small figure receding into the distance. He didn't know just what it was all about, but, judging from what he had just seen, Darla Preston would have a pretty fair-size chore on her hands doing that.

CHAPTER
SIX

Brokaw waited out another minute or two, allowing the worst of the dust to spin away and settle, then clucked the blacks forward. Darla was a rigid, outraged figure at his side. He could hear her quick, labored breathing, then realized how deep and far-reaching her hate for the slim girl was. He waited until they were out of sight beyond the ridge before he spoke.

"From what I heard, I figure you two are not the best of friends. Who is she?"

"Ann Ross," Darla said.

"Double R," Brokaw mused, recalling the brand. "The place is about twenty miles southwest of us. Small, jackleg outfit. Doing no good. Just wasting grass and water."

"Does she run it alone?"

"No. Her brother really owns the place. George Ross. She came here about four years ago from some place in the East. *Humph!* She and her high and mighty ways. I'd like to slap her face."

"You came mighty close . . . with that whip."

"And I would have, too, if you hadn't butted in. I'll thank you, Brokaw, to keep out of my business."

"Had you cut her with that leather, somebody would have been digging a bullet out of you right now, or I'm mighty mistaken about that young woman."

The thought seemed to sober Darla. After a time she said: "I guess she would at that, and welcome the opportunity."

"What's behind all this trouble?"

Darla brushed at her lap and smoothed out a pleat in her skirt. "Are you just curious, or do you really want to know?"

Brokaw said: "I work for Arrowhead. I ought to know who its enemies are, and why."

The iron-tired wheels grating through sand, the steady *clopping* of the trotting blacks, were the only sounds for a minute. Then: "I hear you say that, Brokaw, that fine expression of loyalty, and so on. What I want to know now is do you mean it or are you just talking?"

Brokaw shrugged. "Only a fool tries to play both sides of the table."

At once she turned to him, her face earnest and still. "Brokaw, I meet a man and judge him quick. I think you are what you appear to be, a man that won't back down and that's not afraid to use a gun if need be."

A strange thought came into Frank Brokaw's mind. It had lain, deep and silent, within his subconscious for almost a year, since the search for Matt Slade had begun, in fact. But never before had it reached a point of clarification. Now it was out, facing him, posing its disturbance. Could he ever again kill a man?

Old memories washed back through him, turning him thoughtful and filling him with that vague sickness that brought the sweat out on him. Faint screams and lost yells reëchoed in his ears, and somewhere in the distance a face exploded into a mass of pulp and blood, and guns were booming. Involuntarily he shuddered. Could he kill a man — even Matt Slade? Yes, he could.

"Well?"

He heard Darla Preston's voice and turned to her. "Sorry, I didn't hear."

"You never answered my question," she reminded him. "About the gun."

He said — "I can take care of myself." — and left the matter there.

"We need somebody like that . . . like you at Arrowhead. Oh, I know we've got some tough ones now . . . Shep Russell and Domino, Buckshot Martin, and maybe one or two more. We have to have them to hold what's ours."

"And take what else you want?"

Darla nodded, absolutely honest about it. "And take what we want and need. You asked about the trouble between George Ross and Arrowhead. It started when Ross bought up a few sections of land lying between the two ranches. When he did that, he got control of some of the best wild hay country in this part of the West. Hugh was trying to buy it, too, but he fooled around and let Ross beat him to it. We need that range, need it badly."

"Doesn't Ross?"

94

"He says he does. I don't really know, and it's neither here nor there. All I know is that it's a lot more expensive to raise our beef without it. It causes us to drive our stock clear to Rincon Valley for wintering. If we had that hay meadow country, that expense would be out."

The sun was dropping lower as the day waned. They topped a rise and off in the long distance the darker smudge of Arrowhead, backed against the short hills, became visible.

"George Ross use the meadows?"

"Makes it his winter pasture."

Brokaw shook his head. "Then I guess he needed it when he bought it. Can't blame a man for looking out for himself. And if Prest– ... your husband had a chance to get it but muffed it, you can't very well hold it against Ross."

"Hugh is a fool at times!" Darla exclaimed in an almost savage voice. "But it's land we've got to have, somehow."

"Ever try buying it from Ross?"

"Hugh made him an offer but he wasn't interested. Said he needed it and would keep it."

"Then how do you figure to get it?"

"With men like you," Darla replied blandly. "If he won't sell, we'll force him out and make him give it up. Take it away from him."

Brokaw turned to face her, surprised at the intense quality of her tone. He had a quick recollection of Hugh Preston; he had appeared to be a reasonable sort.

He said then: "Does your husband have the same ideas?"

"Not yet. He's inclined to back away from things like that, from violence. But he will come around to my way of thinking. You say you don't know Hugh. Well, there's little harm in telling you this, because you'll find it out yourself after you've been around for a short while. Hugh's a smart man, almost a brilliant one, but he lacks fire. He doesn't have the push that will make him big and carry him to the top of the heap in this country. And that's where I want him to be."

"And if he doesn't want to go there?"

"Then I'll be there in his place. I'll be on top of the pile."

"What happens then to Hugh Preston?"

"Who cares? He can get out. He can go back where he came from, forget all about being a rancher, and about me."

"Where did he come from?" Brokaw asked casually, taking advantage of the statement.

"Where? Oh, I didn't mean it exactly that way. He wouldn't go back there. Probably move on to California. He's talked about selling out and going there several times."

The shape of Arrowhead's buildings became more definite. Far off to the left, behind the scatter of sheds and buildings, a dust roll marked the passage of cattle as the crew worked them northward.

"What if Hugh won't go for that, either?" Brokaw then said, curious about this frank and forceful woman at his side. "Suppose he won't get out, as you say."

"There'll be no worry about that," she said in a low, confident tone. "It will be my way when the time comes. No matter what Hugh likes, it's what I want that counts. I'll let nothing stand in my way. Nothing."

Brokaw thought over her words, considered the solid, underlying threat of what she had said. There was no weakness there, he decided; she evidently had been planning for some time, and was still carefully laying her groundwork.

"What about Ollie Godfrey?"

Darla skirted a direct reply. "What about him?"

"He seems to have some ideas about being your foreman one of these days soon."

"Ollie has a lot of ideas," she replied with a shrug. "He'd like to be half owner of Arrowhead ... even owner."

"And Abel Cameron?"

"He'll do what Hugh says. Likely he will quit if matters come to a showdown between Hugh and me."

Brokaw frowned. "How far along are your plans?"

"Far enough that I've got to know who's with me and who isn't. If I can't make Hugh see things my way, then I'll take over Arrowhead. By any means and method I find is necessary."

Darla Preston paused. She was looking far ahead, to the buildings of Arrowhead, her eyes dreamy and far-seeing. The afternoon sun reached in under the rig's leather top and glinted off her honey-colored hair, turning her features soft and womanly, a paradox to the strength that lay beneath their smooth surfaces.

"Maybe you think I'm a fool to risk telling you, a total stranger to me, all these things. But I'm not worried. I know men and I know your kind. And I know also that I can make Hugh believe anything I want him to. You try telling him what I've said and I'll deny it, and make you out a liar and have you run off the place."

Brokaw laughed. "You probably could," he said with a faint bitterness.

"Don't make any mistake about it. Just as I said before, nothing stands in my way. Anything or anybody that does will get trampled on."

Brokaw cast a sidelong glance at her. She had not turned her head, but was still lost in a contemplation of Arrowhead. It was difficult to believe such ruthlessness lay behind that calm and beautiful face, that her slim body, with all its gifts, had so great a capacity for hate and violence and greed. Frank Brokaw had known his share of women in his life, but never one like this Darla Preston. She made him think of a gleaming, razor-sharp dagger in a soft, velvet sheath.

"You haven't said where you stand, Brokaw, now that you know the lay of the land."

Brokaw had no intentions of becoming involved in any differences between the Prestons, and certainly he wanted no part of a bloody range war that was sure to follow if the gauntlet was thrown in Ross's face. Anyway, if Preston proved to be Matt Slade, he thought with wry humor he would be doing his part to assist her. The rest would be up to her. But his own needs had to be safeguarded; therefore, it would be wisest to play along.

He said: "You don't think I would be fool enough to tell you I was against you, do you?"

"That's no answer," she retorted. "I want somebody like you backing me up, Brokaw. You're a different breed from the others, from Shep and Domino and their kind. And from Ollie Godfrey, too. They're animals, strong and useful like a good horse, but they lack brains, the ability to think. I like a smart man, one that can see ahead and act, not back down when things get rough. I can make it worth your while."

"Money never interested me much," Brokaw drawled.

"I'm not thinking of money alone. I mean all the other things that go with it . . . half ownership of the ranch. And I go with that."

The forwardness of Darla Preston jarred Brokaw solidly. But a thread of admiration also moved through him. She was a woman steering a course for a high-hung star; she was willing to pay the price, any price to reach it.

He said: "Thanks for the offer. I'll think on it."

"Fine, fine," she murmured. "We'll talk about it again."

CHAPTER
SEVEN

That evening, when supper was through and the crew came straggling into the yard, Ollie Godfrey confronted Brokaw.

"What happened to you last night, drifter? Didn't notice you sleeping in your bunk."

"Never was much of a hand to do my sleeping inside a house," Brokaw replied.

"Could be you think you're too high and mighty to bunk with the rest of the boys."

"Could be," Brokaw said with cool insolence. "Any objections?"

Godfrey was stalled by the candid, bald-faced reply. His mouth tightened and for a moment he appeared inclined to take up the challenge, but it passed quickly. He said: "Thought maybe you'd be taking that advice I gave you."

"Not me," Brokaw said. "Just as I told you, I like it around here."

Two or three men, Shep Russell among them, sidled up beside Godfrey, taking places behind the man. Brokaw twisted up a smoke, indifferent to their hard speculation.

100

"Seems to me you're acting mighty biggity around here," Godfrey said then, apparently heartened by the support he was getting. "That could be a mistake."

"Where you're concerned?" Brokaw said with a short laugh. "I don't think so."

"I'm not alone in this . . . ," Godfrey began angrily.

Brokaw, a match poised between his fingers, swept the group with flat, colorless eyes. "Meaning?"

"Meaning you better watch your step," Godfrey finished "You'd better be watching what you say and what you do. And who you do your talking to."

"I'm scared to death," Brokaw commented dryly, and pushed through the ring of riders, shouldering aside those who stood in his path.

Shep Russell muttered something in a low breath. Brokaw pulled up sharply and wheeled about. He threw a cold, questioning glance at the man. For a long moment Russell met his thrusting gaze, and then looked away. Brokaw laughed, a derisive, harsh sound and, turning back, strolled on into the night.

The clatter of dishes and rattling of pans came from the kitchen where the cook was cleaning up after the evening meal. Several windows of the main house showed light. Brokaw's thoughts came to a full stop upon that. The need to get inside that building, into Hugh Preston's desk and papers, jabbed at him again. There was bound to be something that would furnish a clue to Hugh Preston's previous life. A man would attempt to destroy all things that might possibly indicate his past, but there usually was something, some small item he overlooked, a souvenir, some minor thing, that would be a tip-off. Brokaw knew he had to find it.

But how? How could he gain entrance to the main house and to Preston's desk without raising suspicion? He considered that for a full five minutes, leaning against the rough side of the pole corral. He came eventually to the conclusion that he was hoping for too much, too soon. After all, he had been there but a trifle over one day. Give it a little more time and the opportunity would present itself. As it now stood, he did not actually know where Preston's office was, if indeed he had one. But in all likelihood he did; Preston looked to be the businessman type.

He rolled another cigarette and wandered on by the corral, past the bunkhouse and tool sheds and feed barn. Riders, worn by the day's work in the saddle, were drifting toward their bunks. But sleep was not yet close for him. He reached the end of the yard and halted.

Here the prairie, cool and sweet beneath a silver fog of starlight, rolled away before him to the ragged Sierra Diablos. In their far-off, lifting blur, a coyote laughed into the night and received his echoing reply from a farther distance. Brokaw sighed and rested his length against the rough trunk of an ancient, spreading cottonwood. It was a good thing to be alone now and then. Good to let down the strong guard a man was forced to throw up and maintain against others, against the world. When a man was alone, in the quiet dark, there was time for thinking and old cautions could be tossed to the wind.

★ ★ ★

Darla Preston, dressed in a thin gown over which she had pulled a satin, maroon-colored robe, as beautiful as it was impractical, glanced at her husband. He lounged in deep comfort in one of the heavy leather chairs before the fireplace, smoking his thin, black cigar. Satisfaction blanketed his face, and his entire pose was one of relaxed contentment with everything, with all the world, and this, somehow, angered Darla. It was warm in the big room and the fire in the grate was not at all necessary but Hugh liked it; he enjoyed flames dancing in the stone bank; it catered to his sense of romance.

But the room was stuffy and Darla, a little impatiently, crossed the room and raised one of the windows halfway. She glanced outside. In the gray dusk the new man, Frank Brokaw, stood a little apart from Ollie and four other members of the crew, saying something in that cool, arrogant way of his. He concluded whatever it was, and pushed forward through the men who stepped back to give him room. He was a tall, square-shouldered shape there in the gloom, and Darla watched him in a sort of mesmerized fascination as he halted suddenly, spun about, and again faced the men. He looked, she thought, like a cougar ready to spring.

A moment later, whatever it was that had arrested him passed, and he moved on, disappearing into the shadows beyond the bunkhouse. Darla felt something within her stir. A strong attraction for the dark-faced stranger who had ridden in from nowhere, who came

103

from everywhere, had built itself within her. Something about him frightened her, yet the strong masculinity of him was like a powerful magnet, drawing her to him.

Standing there, watching him glide off, she decided then in that sudden, impulsive way of hers that she would have him with her, at her side, regardless of cost. There was a way to reach Frank Brokaw; there had to be, and she would find it. But one thing she recognized and admitted to herself; he was no child to be wrapped around her finger like Ollie, or some of the other men she had known. He was made of a far different material.

Beauty swayed him not at all. Nor did feminine charm. But it could be done. Darla Preston had yet to meet the man she could not eventually conquer, once she had made up her mind to do it. She trembled a little at the thought, remembering the powerful cut of his body, the way the muscles stood out on his big arms and corded up along his neck, the almost ruthless, irresistible strength in his hands. He made Hugh and Ollie seem no more than children in comparison. Here was a man she could be satisfied with, she thought, as she turned about and moved back into the room.

She faced Hugh, annoyance at his settled complacency, tugging at her lips. "I had more trouble with Ann Ross today," she said by way of bringing up the matter in mind.

Preston glanced up from his cigar. Holding it aside in his thin, tapering fingers, he said: "That so? What happened?"

"She deliberately blocked the road in front of me with a herd of her scrubby cattle. Refused to let me pass."

"Perhaps she had no choice," Preston said mildly. "Steers can be mighty touchy brutes at times."

"Don't you dare defend her!" Darla flared with a great show of anger. "I'm getting sick and tired of all this pussyfooting around where the Ross outfit is concerned. When are you going to do something about them?"

"When the right time comes, Darla. Don't you worry about it."

"When?" she persisted, pinning him down.

"Now, I just can't crack down on George Ross without a good reason, you know that. I've got to have a real good one. Something that will stand up before Ben Marr and the other ranchers around here. George is well liked."

"What do we care about Ben Marr or the other ranchers? That's one of your weak points, Hugh. You don't realize how big and strong Arrowhead is. Nobody would have nerve enough to question anything Arrowhead did."

"Perhaps," Hugh Preston murmured. "But we'll not stampede into something we might later regret. We will take care of the Rosses, but it will be in such a way that there'll be no repercussions. Be patient, dear, the time will come."

"Patient!" Darla's voice lifted almost to a scream. "That's all I have been . . . patient! It's not one of my virtues, Hugh, and I won't stand it much longer. I think you're just stalling, that you're afraid."

Preston flicked the long ash from his cigar into the fireplace. "No," he said slowly, "I'm not afraid. But neither am I a fool. I know when to go slow. You can't want the Double R property any more than I, and I probably realize Arrowhead's need for it far more keenly than anyone else here. I know we will have to have it to survive another bad winter, should one come again. And we shall have the Double R, but it will be done in a way that leaves no black marks."

"If you would get rid of that old man, that Abel Cameron, and put somebody with a little get-up and spunk, like Ollie Godfrey in charge, we might find that good reason you claim to be looking for."

Darla was silent immediately after that. The exasperated outburst had come rushing out, almost before she was aware of it. She had a moment's fear that she had said too much and had overplayed her hand.

Preston stirred, giving her a long, slanting look. "Perhaps you are right," he said reasonably. "Abel is getting old and maybe a bit too careful. But why Godfrey?"

Darla shrugged, making a show of indifference. "No reason particularly. First name that popped into mind. He's strong, maybe a little wild, but the crew looks up to him. I doubt if it would take him long to find a reason for moving in on Ross."

"A point," Preston admitted, getting to his feet. He tossed the cigar butt into the dying fire. "I'll give it some thought." He turned his eyes to her, smiling a little. "Did I tell you it was good to have you home again? This house was lonely while you were gone. I hope you'll not leave it again."

"I hope I never shall," she murmured.

"Coming to bed now? You must be tired."

Darla stepped to his side and gave him a light kiss on the cheek, her manner toward him changing swiftly. "I'm not sleepy. I think I'll sit up for a time. Maybe take a short walk and get some air. You go ahead. I'll be there soon."

"As you wish," Preston said in his polite, formal way. He crossed the room to the door leading into a hallway and the bedrooms beyond. "Good night."

"Good night," she murmured, and watched him pull the door closed. She stepped quickly to it and placed her ear against the paneling. When, moments later, she heard the creak of bedsprings and was satisfied that he had retired, she retraced her footsteps. In the center of the room she hesitated for a moment, doing something with her hair, and then, wheeling, she went to the side door and left the house.

Arrowhead was silent. All lamps were out, even in the kitchen where the cook had finally wound up his chores. Wrapping her robe more tightly about her slim body, she walked quietly along the length of the main ranch house. There she paused to glance about the yard. Assured she was alone, she circled the bunkhouse, passing the bunkhouse, the tool sheds, and feed barn, then coming at last to the stand of trees at the end of the clearing.

Remaining there in the shadows for a moment, she called softly into the night: "Ollie."

He emerged at once from the deep shadows of the grove and hurried to her. She stood quietly resigned, permitting him to take her in his arms, draw her close, and press a kiss upon her lips.

"You took a long time coming," he said.

She pushed him gently away with firm hands. "I was talking with Hugh."

He waited a moment and then said: "He asleep now?"

"Most likely. He went on to bed anyway."

"Then we can talk for a spell."

"For a while. I'm tired, Ollie. I've had a long and hot day. And a long ride."

He stared at her for some time, having his deep thoughts about her. "You seem changed," he said finally. "Anything happen while you were away to change our plans?"

"Nothing."

"Don't let it," Godfrey murmured, his voice carrying a veiled threat. "I won't be cut out of this game now. Not with what you have of mine."

"Don't worry," she replied. "Just be patient. It won't be much longer."

At once he asked: "You talked to Hugh about me?"

"I did. I told him you should be foreman instead of Abel Cameron."

"Did he agree?"

"He will, never fear. But he'll have to think it over, just like he always must."

"And after that, we go ahead with our plans?"

Darla nodded. "Just as we planned. Do you have everything ready? How many men can we depend on?"

Godfrey said: "Four that I'm dead certain of. Maybe five."

"What about the new man . . . Brokaw?"

At once Godfrey said: "We don't want him in on this. We don't want him on Arrowhead at all. I warned him to keep on driftin', and, if he's smart, he'll take the hint."

There was a violence in the man's tone, a strong resentment that lifted his voice to an unnatural tone. Darla, watching him closely, said: "Looks to me like he's the sort we need. Big, tough, and willing to fight anybody for anything."

Godfrey's voice was a soft accusation. "You seem to have got mighty well acquainted with him today."

"He was good company," Darla said, smiling, enjoying the bright flare of jealousy ripping through Godfrey.

"What did he say to you? He try anything? If he did, I'll kill him."

In that same bantering way she observed: "That might be a fair-sized chore for you, Ollie, or for any man. But don't worry. It was an interesting ride, nothing more."

"Dammit," Godfrey breathed hoarsely, turned desperate, not by what she had said, but rather by what she had not. "I wanted to make that trip after you, but old Cameron wouldn't have it that way. I should have gone anyway. I should have told him to go to blazes."

Darla's laugh was a light ripple of sound. "Don't carry on so, Ollie. Nothing happened. We just talked."

"It's a thing I can't help," Godfrey said in a frustrated, whipped voice. "I lost you once, to Hugh Preston. I couldn't stand it again . . . losing you to another man, I mean. If only you'd waited a little while longer for me, Darla."

"I waited as long as I could. I took care of your gold and waited, like I promised. But you never came back, and I thought, finally, the law had caught up with you and you were dead. That was when I married Hugh. But don't worry," she added, laying her hand upon his. "It will be like it was again soon. All that remains is to force Hugh's hand, to get him out of our way. Then, with the money I've kept for you, we'll make Arrowhead the biggest thing in the territory."

"I'll make Hugh move," Godfrey said then in a low, strained tone. "I'll make him. I'll figure out a way to bring it around. Just leave it to me, Darla."

She leaned forward and kissed him. "I know I can rely on you, Ollie. We both want the same thing . . . and we'll have it. You'll see. But you have to make things happen. It's up to you now."

"Don't worry any about it," Godfrey murmured. "I'll find a way. And then everything will go as we planned."

"I'll have to go now," she said after that. "I wouldn't want Hugh to wake up and find me gone. We'll take no chances on having our plans upset."

He moved toward her to claim a farewell kiss, but she turned swiftly away, avoiding his embrace. He groaned, and she heard him wheel away and head toward the bunkhouse, his step slow and dragging. She smiled to herself, thinking of how this man, this Ollie Godfrey was in the cup of her hand. He would do anything she asked, anything she directed him to do. That was exactly the way she wanted him.

Six, or was it seven years ago, she had met Ollie Godfrey — long before Hugh Preston had come into her life. A big, powerful, good-looking man, she had drawn him to her at once and soon had him under her spell. They had made plans, great, towering plans of a life in the West as ranchers, but Ollie had little if any money to make their dreams come true. But he could get it, he had said, and he went away to accomplish just that.

In a few months he was back, bringing the money as he had promised. But he could not stop. There had been some sort of misunderstanding with the law, and it would take time to iron it all out. He left the money with her, exacting her word to keep it safe and wait for his return. But the months passed and he failed to reappear. And then Hugh Preston came along, not one-third the man Ollie Godfrey was, but with plenty of money at his disposal.

And so she had married Hugh and moved into the territory with him. They had purchased the Cresswell place, rebuilt it, and then one day, nearly two years later, Ollie rode into the yard. He was working for George Ross at the Double R, he told her, and he had been searching for her a long time. Now he would claim his own — both Darla and the money he had left in her care. It had taken some fast talking, but in the end she had convinced him that he should hold off, that he should join with her in a bid to gain Arrowhead, then together become the new power in the territory.

She had swayed him as she always could. Now he was in it with her all the way, hand in glove. She would use him as a tool to realize her vaulting ambitions. If he came from the fray unscathed, it would not be so bad. He was a good-looking man; he would make a fine husband. And in either event, she would always end up with his money.

She heard him reach the bunkhouse and enter, allowing the door to slam loudly. There was a grumble of sleepy voices, then it was stone quiet. Moving softly as a shadow, she returned to the main building and entered. Pausing just inside, she listened. A faint snoring came from the bedroom. Hugh was still dead to the world.

CHAPTER
EIGHT

"It'll take well nigh four days runnin'," Abel Cameron was saying the next morning, "so's ye'd best take along your blanket roll. I've got chuck loaded on a pack horse. We won't be drawin' no wagon."

Brokaw, with Godfrey, Shep Russell, Buckshot Martin, and Jack Corbett, turned to make ready for the trip. They were going downcountry a piece to drive back a small herd Preston had purchased from a rancher who was giving up the fight. Godfrey was not liking it, and was saying as much as he walked with the other members of the crew toward the bunkhouse.

But Cameron was a firm man. Thirty minutes later they rode from the yard, striking due south, with the rising sun at their left shoulders. They spoke little, each man having his own far-reaching thoughts and keeping them to himself. Cameron, trailing the pack horse with a short length of rope, was somewhat apart from the others. Brokaw slanted across to him.

Before he could speak, the old foreman said: "Not smart, me bringin' you along with Shep and Ollie and his bunch, but there weren't nobody else around. Now, see they's no trouble. You hear?"

Brokaw said: "If there's any trouble, they will be the ones who start it. Much of a herd we're after?"

Cameron shook his head. "Not much. Twelve hundred head or so Mister Preston told me."

"You figure to stop in town on the way?"

Cameron's faded gaze swung to the tall rider. "You got business there?"

"Not me," Brokaw replied. "Just heard the boys talking. It's been a long time since they bellied up to a bar, according to what they said."

Cameron studied the distant hills for a moment, his wind-scoured features sharp against the lifting light. "Well, I reckon it wouldn't do no harm, lettin' them wet their whistles. Ain't none out of the way."

Brokaw nodded his agreement and satisfaction. He had been hoping for just such an opportunity to talk with the foreman. After a shot glass or two of whiskey, or a few beers, most men opened up a little. Maybe he could learn a few things about Hugh Preston. The bits of information garnered here and there were beginning to tote up, but he needed more to make it conclusive.

"Want me to pass the word on?"

"No," Cameron said sagely, "you tell 'em now and they'll bust a gut gettin' into town so's they can have a little more time. We got no spare horses along and I don't figure to have what we got run ragged. I'll tell 'em when we get there."

But Ollie Godfrey had ideas of his own. When they were still a long five miles from Westport Crossing, he and Shep Russell suddenly disappeared behind a roll of low hills. Cameron, seeing this, waved the others in.

114

"Reckon we'll stop off in town for a hour or so," he announced. "But don't go gettin' likkered up. I'm tellin' you now, any man that does, is fired."

Buckshot Martin threw his pig eyes toward the point where Godfrey and Russell had dropped from sight in a meaningful way. "Thanks," he murmured dryly, and wheeled away, Corbett following him closely.

It was fully 10:00 a.m. when they turned into the end of the town's single street and rode up to the rail in front of the Longhorn. The four other Arrowhead horses were already there. Brokaw swung down and Cameron followed, more slowly and somewhat stiffly. The old foreman, by all rules, should not have attempted the trip. He could have sent a younger man in his place, but the iron-headedness of him refused to accept any limitations of advancing age, and he stubbornly resisted all intimations that he should follow an easier course of activity for himself.

Brokaw looped the leathers over the tie bar and turned about. He came to a complete halt, seeing Ann Ross pull up in a light buckboard directly across the street. For a moment their eyes locked and Brokaw saw, or thought he saw, the faintest greeting in her eyes. He touched the brim of his wide-brimmed hat and ducked his head. Ann, trim and fresh-looking in gingham, turned swiftly away.

"Mighty fine little filly," Cameron observed from the far side of Brokaw's horse. "Didn't know you was acquainted."

"We've met," Brokaw said shortly and stepped up onto the Longhorn's porch.

115

He shouldered through the scarred batwing doors of the saloon, holding them back for Cameron to enter. The place was empty except for the bartender and the quartet of Arrowhead riders who were sitting at a far table, a bottle and glasses before them. Cameron bent his steps toward them.

"Now, I'm warnin' all of you, take it easy with that bottle. I'll put up with no drunks on this drive."

"All right, grampa," Godfrey said broadly. "We'll sure be good boys."

Cameron eyed the cowpuncher closely. " 'Pears to me you already had aplenty, Ollie."

"Sure, sure," Godfrey replied, and deliberately poured himself another liberal drink.

Cameron's lined face hardened and the skin, stretched over his cheek bones, whitened. He reached across the table and slapped the glass from Godfrey's fingers, sending it clattering across the floor.

The whiskey splattered Buckshot Martin. He yelled and pushed back his chair. Godfrey, eyes blazing, leaped to his feet, hand going for his gun.

Brokaw's level voice snapped through the confusion. "Hold it, Ollie!"

Godfrey hesitated, his poised, half-crouched shape going rigid. "Stay out of this," he snarled. "The old man's been asking for it for a long time. Don't buy into something you can't handle!"

"I can handle it," Brokaw said quietly. "Now get out of here. You heard Cameron say you'd had plenty. Looks that way to me, too. I reckon he meant it."

116

Cameron shifted angrily. "Now, wait a minute there, Brokaw. I can run my own affairs without no . . ."

"Sure," Brokaw agreed easily. But there was no relaxing of his attention upon Godfrey and the others. He waited out the moments, his cold glance covering them all, then Godfrey shrugged.

"Let's go," he said, and started toward the doorway, the rest trooping obediently after him.

Only then did the coiled readiness of Frank Brokaw fade. He faced the bartender and ordered a glass of beer. Abel Cameron moved up beside him and repeated the request, and together they walked to a table and sat down.

Anger still fanned Cameron's pale eyes. "I'd appreciate your stayin' out of my business," he said tartly. "I reckon I can look after myself. Been doin' it for a mighty long spell now."

Brokaw said: "I know that. But look at the odds you were up against. Four to one. I don't cotton to that kind of fight."

Cameron's fierce pride was somewhat mollified. "I reckon it was at that. Russell and Buckshot would sure side Ollie, once he started somethin'. And probably Jack would do the same, when he saw which way the wind was blowin'."

He took a sip of the beer, relenting another notch. Wiping the edges of his mustache with a bony hand, he said: "Goes right good after a dusty ride." Then: "That Ollie's lookin' for trouble all the time."

"He'll find it one of these days," Brokaw commented.

Cameron wagged his head. "He sure will that. Proddy as a spring bull. Is he givin' you any trouble?"

"None I can't take care of," Brokaw replied. It was a subject made to order for him. He said: "Known him long?"

"Three, four years. He used to work for George Ross but quit him and started workin' for us. He was some sweet on that little Ross gal, I hear tell."

Brokaw considered this information for a moment. Ollie really got around, so far as women were concerned. "You've been foreman for Arrowhead ever since Preston bought the place," he said, sticking to the original subject. It was a statement rather than a question.

Cameron nodded. "I was foreman for Cresswell when he sold out to Preston. I went with the sale."

"About five years ago, I guess."

"Closer to six."

"Where did Preston come from?"

Cameron took another swallow of the warm beer. "Don't rightly know. Seems I heard it was Nebrasky, or maybe it was Wyomin'. Why? You heard of him before?"

"Can't say," Brokaw replied slowly. "Name's a little familiar. Did he used to ride a big red sorrel and set a real fancy saddle, one that was all dolled up with silver?"

Cameron gave that some lengthy thought. Then: "You lookin' to find a man like that, son? Is that what you're doin' in this country?"

Brokaw smiled ruefully to himself. He should have guessed he could not fool the old foreman for long. He shrugged. "Just trying to place him."

118

Cameron said: "Well, if it's any help to you, I don't recollect seein' Preston on no red horse, nor forkin' any fancy silver saddle, either. Not since I knew him, anyway. Best I recall him and his missus showed up in a surrey all loaded down with her duds and things like that. 'Course, he could have shucked his horse and saddle before he came here."

Brokaw said: "Preston came with a lot of money, they tell me."

"Plenty. He sure fixed up the old Arrowhead. 'Twas about on its last legs when he bought it up." He finished off his drink and got to his feet. "Reckon we better be moseyin'. Wonder where Ollie and them other waddies meandered off to."

"Likely waiting at the horses," Brokaw answered, and flipped a coin to the bartender.

They crossed the saloon's broad width and came up to the doors. Glancing over their tops, Brokaw saw Martin and Corbett leaning against the tie rail. They were watching the batwings with sharp, expectant interest, as if anticipating something unusual and entirely to their liking. Brokaw pressed a hand against Cameron's shoulder, halting him. Motioning for silence, he eased to the far side of the entrance and, bending low, threw his gaze to the outside. He saw the booted feet of a man on the porch, standing close to the door frame. He checked the opposite side. There, another pair of legs awaited them.

Pulling back into the saloon, he whispered to Cameron: "We've got a reception committee. Wait here."

119

"Ollie?"

"Ollie and Shep."

"Let's take the back door," Cameron suggested.

Brokaw's mouth split into a wicked grin. "Might as well let them have their fun."

He stepped softly to the swinging doors and placed a hand, palm first against each. With a sudden, hard push he swung them outward. Immediately he jerked them back in. Shep Russell, caught by the false move, lunged — thinking Brokaw was stepping into the open. He saw his error, tried to catch himself, failed, and went stumbling off. Brokaw, coming then through the batwings, drove him to his knees with a vicious, chopping blow. Brokaw moved quickly onto the porch then, pivoting to meet Godfrey who came rushing in.

He took a wild, roundhouse swing high on the shoulder and then returned a sizzling right that cracked against the cowboy's head. Godfrey grunted and grabbed frantically for him. Brokaw knocked his reaching hands aside, then smashed him hard in the face, twice. Shep Russell was struggling to get up, resting uncertainly on his hands and knees, breathing hard. Brokaw placed his foot against the man's ribs, shoved, and sent him rolling off the porch into the dust of the street.

He became aware then of shouts, of men attracted by the fight, pounding up to watch. He saw Ann Ross across the way, on the doorstep of MacGillivray's general store, her face a tan oval of suppressed excitement as she looked on. Godfrey's knuckles smashed into his jaw and he staggered back a step. The

120

cowboy came weaving in, his eyes wild, his face set, anxious to finish it up. Brokaw, not napping now, met him coming. He stalled him with a stiff left. Godfrey wavered on his heels and off balance. Brokaw drove a hard right wrist deep into his belly. Wind gushed from Godfrey's mouth. His eyes popped out in pain and he buckled forward. Staggering backward, he missed the edge of the porch and piled up in the street.

A shout lifted among the spectators. Cameron's worried, insistent voice cut through the dust and swirling confusion. "Get on them horses! Ben Marr'll have the whole bunch of you in the calaboose in another minute."

Brokaw and Cameron moved to Godfrey's side and dragged him to his feet. Half carrying him, they loaded him onto his saddle and jerked the reins free of the rail. The other riders were already aboard and moving off. Cameron swung up, and Brokaw stepped to his own horse. With the sick and heaving Godfrey between them, they started down the street at a fast walk.

Brokaw, remembering Ann Ross, threw a quick glance toward her. She had come farther out onto the porch and was watching him with an odd mixture of admiration and revulsion in her dark eyes. He grinned through his bruised lips and she swung quickly around, placing her back to him. Even from that angle, he thought, she was a mighty good-looking woman.

Ann Ross felt her cheeks burning when she turned from Brokaw's bold glance. It angered her to realize how this tall dark-faced man affected her, attracting her almost against her will it seemed, and stirring something deep inside her. She met Cornelius MacGillivray's steady eyes with a defiant look.

The grizzled old storekeeper smiled knowingly. "That one is quite a man, eh, lass?"

"I'm sure I wouldn't know, and care less," she retorted, and flounced back into the store's musty depths.

MacGillivray chuckled, following her slim shape with his wise old eyes.

"I would like to get on with my list, if you please," she said with a great display of formality.

And MacGillivray, the ghost of a smile still playing about his colorless lips, said: "Of course, of course."

An hour later, boxed supplies in the bed of the buckboard, she again considered the darkly sunburned stranger called Frank Brokaw. Since that day on the road, when she had first seen him with Darla Preston, she had not been entirely successful in getting his broad-shouldered image out of her mind. He looked to be the usual sort Preston hired to work Arrowhead's vast holdings, and, yet, he was not one of them. There was none of the ordinary, every-day hardcase toughness about him; there was instead a deep-lying violence that bespoke a steady purpose of some sort — all of which had an overlay of ironic humor.

She remembered the flat grayness of his eyes when he had been driving his balled fists into Ollie Godfrey in that terrible, relentless way, the slight upcurling of his long lips when he had booted Shep Russell into the dust. It had been a different look that day on the trail when he had stayed Darla's hand on the whip. The amusement had been apparent then, as if he considered her actions those of a small and badly spoiled child, to be tolerated within certain bounds. She wondered what he thought of Darla, if he was to be another of her conquests, as had been Ollie and the others before him, who had found favor with her.

Certainly he would be the type Darla would turn her charms on. She would go all out for a big, handsome man like Brokaw, and be all the more determined to have him if he showed any signs of resistance or disinterest. That was the way she had been with Ollie; she had simply set out to have him, it seemed, to take him away from the Double R — and Ann. And she had quickly done so. Ann could think about it now. At first it had hurt a little but, she realized, affairs such as theirs had not been truly fated and the hurt had healed fast. Eventually she was actually glad Darla had won.

But Darla might not find it so easy with Frank Brokaw. He didn't look the sort who would jump every time Darla cried frog. He would do what he pleased, just when it pleased him, and Ann found herself hoping he would stay that way. Then, being Ann Ross and the honest sort of person she was, she wondered why any of it should make any difference to her.

Only, she assured herself, because she was sick of Darla Preston's making a fool of every man who rode into the Scattered Hills country. And of Hugh. Poor Hugh. He wasn't a bad sort, really. But so blind! He didn't know half of what went on at Arrowhead. He was like so much clay in Darla's hands, so completely

123

overcome by her charm and physical attributes that he could not think beyond them. If only he knew. But just as it was true in most cases of that sort, he would be the last to know.

The sun was high and hot. Ann pulled under a broad, spreading cottonwood, leafed out almost to full dress, to give the horses a breather. She dabbed at her forehead with a square of folded linen and wiped the circle of her mouth.

Glancing at the cloth, she grimaced at the smudge of dust, smiling then at what the young ladies of Miss Vale's School for Gentlewomen in St. Louis would think, if they could but see her in that moment.

Too bad Frank Brokaw had not come by Double R first in his quest for a job, if indeed that was what had brought him there. They could use a man like Brokaw. He looked like he was able to hold his own with any man, under any condition. And he could probably use that gun slung at his hip just as effectively. She gave a small sigh. Riders seeking work always went first to Arrowhead. The power of the big spread drew them as surely as honey brought flies and what Preston did not hire, the culls and the rag-tail drifters and leftovers, fell to the small, less prominent ranches like the Double R.

But it would be nice to have a man like Brokaw working on the place. It would give the place a sense of stability, of being able to stand proud and alone, if necessary. He would make a good foreman. George would say they couldn't afford it but it might pay off in the long run. The percentage of calf drop had fallen last year and looked like it would be much worse this season. And there was no accounting for it, openly that was. But a good foreman like Brokaw would soon get to the bottom of it and straighten it out.

She decided then to talk to her brother about it, visualizing in that moment the reaction of Darla Preston if such a thing came to pass. Darla did not take kindly to defeat of any kind, particularly where her men were concerned. But Ann didn't care. They actually needed a man like Frank Brokaw on the Double R. In her next thought she amended that: they needed Frank Brokaw.

CHAPTER
NINE

He had learned little, if anything of value from Abel Cameron. Brokaw admitted that to himself early the morning of the fourth day, when they reached that indefinite boundary of Arrowhead range with the new herd. He did not think the foreman was holding back on him; he just didn't have any information that was of use.

Sitting ramrod straight on the bay, he let his eyes travel out over the herd, strung in an elongated triangle along the floor of the shallow valley through which they were moving. In the dusty haze he could see Abel Cameron, riding ahead at point position, a hundred yards or so in lead of the first steer. It had been an easy drive. At the very beginning, a red-eyed old longhorn, gaunt and brush-scarred, had forged his arrogant head to the fore and taken charge. From then on it was merely a matter of keeping the knobby-kneed brute pointed in the right direction, and prodding the laggards to keep up.

Brokaw was glad the drive was about over with. Not that he disliked the saddle, but it was preventing him from fulfilling his avowed purpose, from the completion of that relentless, pressing desire to find Matt Slade and bring him to account. Almost a week now, he mused, and only small progress had been made.

True, Hugh Preston seemed to fill most of the requirements — and yet he did not, factually. Everything was circumstantial, nothing positive. And Brokaw knew he must be sure before he played his last ace. One wrong move and Hugh Preston would cover quickly and be gone like a startled covey of mountain quail.

But something must be done soon. Past experience had taught Brokaw it was never wise to remain overly long in one place. Lawmen, by their very nature, had a habit of becoming curious about him and his intentions, just as had Ben Marr. He was glad they had got out of Westport Crossing that day of the fight, before the old sheriff had showed up.

Thinking of Ollie Godfrey, he threw a glance to the tail end of the herd where he along with Shep Russell and Buckshot Martin were holding down the drag points. Corbett, like himself, was at swing, directly across on the opposite side of the herd. There had been no more trouble from either Ollie or Shep. Except for a glowering look from Godfrey on different occasions, there was no further reference made to the affair in front of the Longhorn. But Godfrey was not forgetting it, he knew. He was the kind that could not accept defeat and live with it; he would carry the thought of it in his breast until it became a festering sore, forever looking for the moment when he might vindicate himself in the eyes of others, as well as his own.

Later on, when they were not more than a half dozen miles from Preston's buildings, Brokaw caught sight of an approaching horseman. It was too far to tell who it was. He watched as the rider angled across the range to where Cameron plodded along, halted him, and engaged in a few minutes conversation. Then the rider swung away, swinging around the boil of dust, heading toward him. He saw then that it was Darla Preston.

She approached at an easy canter, riding her horse with a calm expertness. She was wearing a silky tan riding habit, a jaunty hat perched high on her blonde hair, and a spider-web veil that shadowed her face and gave it a sort of mysterious, brooding quality. She was riding side-saddle. Brokaw remembered a picture he once saw in a magazine, showing an Eastern lady of quality sitting her mount in just such elegant fashion. It was a bit incongruous, here on the range; where most women and girls donned split riding skirts, or drew on their menfolk's castoff Levi's and shirts, and forked a regular stock saddle. But it made a fetching picture. She waved gaily to him as she pulled in alongside the gelding. He touched the brim of his hat, quite frankly admiring her appearance.

"Like what you see?" she asked archly.

Brokaw grinned. "A picture any man would."

She laughed coolly. "Made up your mind about my offer?"

Brokaw made no reply. The herd was moving steadily past. Over his left shoulder he saw Godfrey and the others on a direct line with them now. Godfrey was watching Darla with sharp, mistrusting eyes.

128

He said: "Yes."

"I'm glad," she answered at once. "I need you, Brokaw. Need your help."

"Don't figure on it."

She turned to him. "I don't understand. You mean you aren't coming in with me?"

"That's right. Don't count on me."

Darla gave a little start. Her face flushed beneath its fragile shield and a hurrying, brief hardness stiffened it, setting it into unlovely angles. And as quickly it changed again. Her full lips parted into a smile. "You are so very positive. But I'm no hand at taking no for an answer. I think you will change your mind," she said, and with a flick of her hand whirled about and rode toward Arrowhead.

Brokaw threw a quick glance at Godfrey, now less than fifty yards distant. The cowboy was watching Darla leave, his jaw grim and set. She had not bothered to notice him, not even deigning to wave when she departed. Brokaw came back around; Darla was a small shape now far in the distance. His eyes then caught the bit of white lying on the ground near where she had stopped. He clucked the bay closer and, leaning from the saddle, scooped it up. It was one of her gloves, slim, expensively worked doeskin, with the faint odor of her lilac perfume clinging to it.

He stared at it for a long time, having his thoughts about it. She had dropped it deliberately, of course. That was evident. And she believed he would return it to her at a place where she could be found after the ranch was quiet. He smiled and tucked it into his shirt pocket. He would return it all right, but not in the way she had planned. He had needed an excuse to get inside the ranch house and locate Hugh Preston's desk. Now he had it.

Not long after supper that evening he crossed the yard and rapped at the side door of the log building. It was opened at once by Preston, who nodded his greetings, and invited him to enter.

"What can I do for you, Frank?"

It was odd the rancher should remember his first name but some men were like that. His eyes reached beyond Preston into the room, cluttered with heavy, comfortable furniture, brightly colored Indian rugs, elk and deer head trophies on the walls. No desk was to be seen. He withdrew the glove from his pocket.

"Found this on the range this afternoon," he said, handing the doeskin to Preston. "Figured it was your wife's and that she'd like to have it back."

The rancher accepted the glove, turning it over and over in his thin fingers. "Why, I believe it is hers. Just a moment, I'll call her."

Preston moved across the room toward a door that led off into a hallway. Brokaw drifted closer to the fireplace, eyes probing his surroundings. There was no saddle, silver or otherwise in sight, but he did locate the desk. A small porch, on the front of the house, had been converted into an office. The desk, a huge roll-top affair, stood against its north wall. A door opened off, leading into the yard bordering the front of the structure. There was one window, small and high off the ground.

130

"Brokaw," Preston said, coming back into the room, "my wife says it is hers and to extend her thanks to you for bringing it in. She lost it sometime today when she rode out to see the stock I bought."

"My pleasure," Brokaw murmured. He glanced up to see Darla standing well back of Preston in the depths of the narrow hallway. Her face was still and she was watching him, disconcerted and seemingly at a loss at his behavior.

He turned away then, deliberately choosing the door off the office, and went through it. It led into the yard at the front, as he had suspected. He circled the building, crossing in front of the bunkhouse, and made his way to the barn where he still bunked alone. There he waited until everything had grown quiet, and then returned to the yard.

Drawing off a short distance in to the shadows back of the main house, he spent another hour watching and smoking his cigarettes. Finally deeming it safe, he went to the door of Preston's office. It was unlocked as he had thought it would be. He let himself in quietly and stood there for a time in the utter darkness, listening. Lights had been out for some time, but he had to be certain neither Darla nor Hugh Preston was still up, was there in the front parlor lost to his view in the depths of the heavy furniture. Darla, he knew, had not left the building. She had expected him to meet her at the grove, and, when he chose to ignore the invitation, she had remained inside. He wondered then if Ollie was there, waiting.

131

Convinced that all was safe, he went to Preston's desk. He dared not light a lamp, but used innumerable matches instead, shielding them with a cupped hand to keep their glare from reaching beyond the room. There was little in the desk. Account books, tally records, bills, all orderly and neatly placed. He examined every drawer, many of which were empty. He thought then that there must be a safe or some such depository where valuables were kept, but a search of the room failed to turn it up. When he had finished, he had found nothing of interest, nothing that would indicate Hugh Preston was anyone other than Hugh Preston, and the disappointment turned him still and thoughtful.

But it was inconclusive, he told himself as he slipped back into the yard. Any man wishing to bury the past would use extreme care in destroying all things that might link him to another life. He half smiled then, remembering he had given himself that same assurance before. But the inherent honesty and fairness of the man insisted that he be sure, that he be dead certain before he took a life.

He reëntered the barn, glancing again to the back room where the equipment was kept. He had examined the gear before but he checked it again, thinking some additions might have been made. A flaring match revealed no silver saddle.

He pinched out the match and paused in the blackness of the stable. It had to be Hugh Preston. Slade and Preston were one and the same and somewhere there was proof of it. But time was growing short. He decided then to give it a couple of more days, three at the most, and then, if he had uncovered nothing conclusive, he would load Hugh Preston on a horse and take him clear to Central City. It might prove to be a fair-size job, but it would have to be done. Once in Central City, Tennyson, the banker could make the identification, could finally say Preston was Slade.

CHAPTER
TEN

"Pair off," Abel Cameron said that morning at the finish of breakfast, "and work out all them draws and cañons on the east slope of the hills. They're full up with beef hid out there in the brush, and the only way we're goin' to get them down for roundup is to pop 'em out."

Frank Brokaw borrowed a pair of the foreman's leather chaps and joined the half dozen riders assigned the disagreeable task. They rode across the low swells of the range with the sun at their backs — Godfrey, Russell, Jules Strove, the man called Domino, Jack Corbett, and Brokaw. They were slanting for the rough slopes of the Sierra Diablos, a rugged world of loose rock, buckthorn, piñon, scrub oak, and deep slashes.

When they reached the first outcroppings of badlands, Brokaw found himself lined up with Strove. Godfrey and his ever-present shadow, Shep Russell, had swung away, choosing the lower, more easily worked areas. Domino and Corbett were near them, only slightly higher.

"'Pears the boys left the easy part for us," Strove murmured laconically, his glance sweeping the ragged territory of the upper climes. "I misdoubt if ary a goat

134

would figure to live up there. But now, a longhorn, he's different. An old mossy'd figured that was pure heaven up there, and I calculate we'll have us a time gettin' what's up there down to the bottom."

Brokaw grinned his agreement and together they started the steep climb.

They rode for thirty minutes and then paused to allow their winded horses to rest. The little hoop-legged rider, hunching against a piñon, drew the makings from his pocket and rolled a lumpy cigarette. Cocking his head to one side, he said: "You see Miz Preston yestiddy, Brokaw? She was sure some fixed up. Reckon she's about the femalest woman I ever set my peepers on."

"For a fact," Brokaw said.

"You figure she was ever a stage woman? Don't hardly seem like no regular gal would know how to fix herself up like Miz Preston does."

"Do you have any other reason for thinking she might have been an actress?" Brokaw was immediately alert. Here might be some indication of Hugh Preston's background.

"Nope," Strove said, rising to his feet. "Just don't seem nacheral for a regular woman to fix up and dress the way she does. Takes a lot of know-how, same as everything else."

The going was tough. Stiff brush plucked at them, and the buckskin Brokaw had picked for the day was having a hard time of it. They wormed slowly up the slope, snaking back and forth to make it easier on the horses. They reached a small basin hemmed in with a solid ring of scrub oak. Two steers watched them approach with wild, bloodshot eyes, but Jules Strove sailed right on into the clearing at them — yelling at the top of his lungs, and waving his doubled rope overhead. The long-horns bolted and went crashing through the leafy barrier, headed for lower ground. Strove rode their tails until he spotted Jack Corbett at the next level.

"Cowboy, here's your babies!" he yelled at the redhead, and turned back.

He rejoined Brokaw and they pushed slowly on, working out every thicket, each hollow. Strove, a little way below Brokaw, commented: "Reckon we ain't goin' to jump any she-stuff up here. Only old mossyhorns, too dang' ornery to bed with the herd, will pick this place."

If Godfrey and the other riders had deliberately picked the lower part of the hills for easier going, they were getting the most activity. Watching the small shapes of the riders, Brokaw could see them weaving in and out of the brush, chousing cattle at regular intervals. Godfrey seemed to have assumed the lead of the entire operation, however, and had pulled completely off the slope proper, and was riding the smoother shoulder of the rangeland.

"Just like old Ollie," Strove observed dourly. "He's too cussed purty to get hisself scratched up."

They routed out a half dozen more steers, all singles, and drove them down to the man below. It was near noon when they came unexpectedly upon a narrow, dead-end cañon. In a clearing at the center, in a space no larger than a wagon bed, they met up with an old

136

renegade longhorn. No victim of the knife and dabbing stick, he was an escapee of a half dozen roundups and he now prepared to maintain that record. He was an old blue with a multitude of scars patching his hide, and a six-foot spread of needle-pointed horns. He greeted the two riders with lowered head.

"Watch that one," Brokaw warned.

The old blue snorted and rolled his red eyes. His tail switched back and forth, snapping like a leather whip.

"Bastard's so old he wouldn't even make good taller," Strove said. "Howsomever, Abel said to bring them all in."

Holding his rope folded double to shape a whip, he yelled and drove spurs into his pony. The bull spun away, blowing loudly through widely flaring nostrils. Strove's horse reached the clearing, wild and jumpy from the cowboy's yells and jabbing spurs. Brokaw, coming in from the opposite side, added his own shouts and the longhorn plunged off into the screen of piñon.

"Head him downslope!" Strove cried.

Brokaw was already behind the bull that was moving, fast and quiet, as only a wily old longhorn can do when he sets his mind to it.

"*Hi yah! Hi yah!*" Strove's voice sang. "Git along, you danged old rebel!"

He was crowding the bull close, too close. Brokaw yelled a warning but it came too late. The bull wheeled, almost rearing upright on his hind legs. Dead branches and leaves exploded in front of him and he was suddenly charging back at Strove.

The cowboy yelped. His horse came up, unseating him. He struck on his feet and bolted for the brush while his pony scampered frantically out of the path of the bull. Brokaw, a half dozen steps away, drew his gun and snapped a hasty shot into the ground ahead of the steer. The longhorn plowed to a halt, whirled again, and thundered off into the brush.

"Gol danged stinkin' son-of-Satan!" Strove raved. "I'll pusonnaly see that critter gets to the slaughterin' chute, even if I have to ride a cattle car all the way to the packin' house!" Strove recovered his jittery horse and climbed back into the saddle. "I'll nudge him out," he said, his eyes on the brush into which the blue had escaped. "You go on ahead. I'll catch up."

Two rapid gunshots drifted hollowly up from the range. Brokaw, sweating a little from the last moments' excitement, rode forward to a projecting ledge from which he could look down.

"Maybe that old blue devil's already reached the bottom," Strove said, half hopefully, turning his horse to follow Brokaw.

Godfrey and the three other Arrowhead riders had drawn off a short distance from the brushy lip of the slope. Three other riders were facing them over a short space while a small jag of cattle milled around behind them.

"Looks like trouble down there," Strove said.

Brokaw nodded. "Let's take a look."

They rode down the slope, finding a trail that made the descent fairly easy. Brokaw, his glance on the three outsiders, quickly recognized one — Ann Ross. The other two were men he had never seen before, but one was surely Ann's brother George. The other was likely one of their cowpunchers.

"Look what we caught!" Godfrey chortled as they came up. "Real, genuine rustlers!"

The dark eyes of the big man snapped. He was graying at the temples and his mouth was a hard line. "What are you talking about, Godfrey? We're hunting strays same as you."

"On Arrowhead range?" Godfrey came back with a knowing lift of his brows.

Brokaw's gaze settled upon Ann Ross. A worried frown puckered her brow and drew her lips into a small, compressed circle; her face had paled beneath its tan. Brokaw shifted his attention to Godfrey and the other Arrowhead men; the incident apparently was far more serious than he had surmised. Faint echoes of Darla Preston's words came back to Brokaw — don't miss any chances, make something happen — or words to that effect had been her orders to Godfrey. This moment had some relation to that command, he realized.

"Ann, ride on home."

Brokaw swiveled his glance to the speaker, the big man on the bay. He could see the resemblance to Ann now, the same deeply shadowed eyes, the identical firm jaw and chin. And he was struck by another thought; George Ross fitted very well the description he had of Matt Slade. He searched back through his memory — when did they say Ross had come into this country? Six years ago? The number seemed to stick in his mind but he was not sure. Yet it was something like that. And that would place his arrival at about the time Slade was supposed to have come.

Ann shook her head. "I'll not leave."

George Ross said: "This looks like trouble and I'll not have you hurt."

"I'll stay," Ann replied stubbornly.

"Sure, let her stay," Shep Russell said with a wide grin. "She's part of the same thievin' outfit. Give her some of the same medicine."

"Lay a hand on her, any of you, and I'll kill you," Ross said in a low, savage voice.

"You won't be in no shape to do anything," Ollie Godfrey remarked, "when we get finished with you. Mister Preston don't stand for no rustling on his range, and I figure he expects us to do something about it when we come across it being done."

"What do you mean, rustling?" George Ross demanded hotly. "We're busting out strays, just like you are. A good bit of my stock's drifted onto Preston's range during the winter. Likely there's some Arrowhead stuff on Double R, too."

"Why don't you wait until roundup? Don't you trust us?" Godfrey asked in a smirking voice.

"Sure, I trust Arrowhead, but we knew this bunch was in here and there was no sense in driving them clear across Preston's range and then having to go after them later."

Ollie Godfrey pointed to one of the steers in the group Ross had been herding. "Looks like an Arrowhead brand on that critter."

Ross nodded. "Probably some more in there, too, along with my own. You didn't give us a chance to cut them out. You jumped us before we were finished with them."

"Oh, sure," Godfrey said, "you were just going to cut out your branded stuff and leave the rest here waiting for us."

"That's exactly right," George Ross said.

"In a pig's eye," Godfrey snorted. "Come dark that bunch of cows would've been mixed in your herd and in another week they'd been wearing a new brand . . . Double R."

Ross said: "You know better than that, Ollie. You know I've never rustled a head of cattle in my life."

"Man's got to start sometime. Looks like you've done just that."

Brokaw saw the anger flame across Ross's face and his hand drop to the gun at his hip.

"Don't do it, George!" Godfrey barked. "It's six to your two, not counting your sister. You wouldn't have a chance."

"What's all the jawin' for, Ollie?" Shep Russell broke in then. "They ain't nothin' but rustlers. Why ain't we treatin' them like rustlers, instead of doing all this palavering?"

"I'm coming to that," Godfrey replied. He threw his glance along the slope. "No tree fit for a hanging party around here. Guess we'll have to do the next best thing." He swung his gaze to Ann. "You sure you want to stick around here? This won't be pretty."

Brokaw saw Ann's eyes lift to him, bright with their unspoken plea for help. Their gaze held for a moment, and then she looked away, back to Godfrey. "You wouldn't dare hurt us, Ollie."

"Law's the law," Godfrey said with a shrug. "It says a rustler's got to be strung up. We got no trees big enough so we'll have to work it another way."

Jules Strove broke in. "You sure you know what you're doin'?"

"You bet your life I do," Godfrey shot back. "And if there's any of you that don't agree with me, just ride on off and go about your business!" He allowed his eyes to come to a stop on Brokaw, his meaning plain. Brokaw watched him with a cold detachment.

Godfrey drew his gun and leveled it at Ross. "Shep, you and Domino tie their hands behind them. Then take their ropes and hitch them to the saddle. I reckon a little dragging over these rocks will be about the same as hanging."

There was a long moment of complete hush following that, and then Ann's scream broke the silence. She spurred forward, grabbing for the gun in her brother's holster. Shep Russell threw himself against Ross, blocking her off. He lifted his hand and struck her across the shoulder. Ross tried to spin away, to help her, but Domino caught him against the flank of his own horse and pinned him to the saddle. Russell, laughing, seized Ann by the arm and began to pull her off her pony.

Brokaw had seen enough. "Take your hands off her, Shep!" His voice cut through the confusion.

Godfrey and the other Arrowhead riders swung quickly to face him. He was sitting quietly in the saddle, his gun on Godfrey.

"Put that iron away, Ollie. And the rest of you, don't get any ideas. We'll just hold this thing up a minute or two. What Ross says seems reasonable to me."

"Damn you, don't you cut in on this," Godfrey said in a tight, rasping voice.

"I'm not standing by and see two men murdered just to please you," Brokaw snapped. "Jules," he called to the cowboy waiting off to his right, "take a look at that stock Ross gathered up! See how much of it is Double R stuff."

Strove rode forward and made his inspection. In a few minutes he reported: "'Most all Ross stock. I see only two, three Arrowhead."

"So what?" Godfrey demanded. "One steer's all it takes to make a man a rustler."

"Depends," Brokaw interjected. "Depends a lot on who the man might be. Right now I think you're all wrong, Ollie. If Ross wanted to rustle some of Preston's beef, he could find it in a lot handier place than here, in this brush pile."

Ross, silent through it all, said: "If I wanted to, that's true. But there's never been an Arrowhead steer on my ranch unless he drifted over of his own notion. And Preston always got him back. Which is more than I can say about some of the stuff of mine that has wandered onto Arrowhead range."

"That I don't know anything about," Brokaw said. "Preston's the man to take that up with." He threw a glance to Strove. "Cut those Arrowhead steers out, Jules, and head them back up the way."

Strove immediately fell to work, hazing the stock that bore Preston's brand out of the bunch.

In a strained, angered voice Godfrey said: "You'll be sorry for this, Brokaw. You've stuck your nose into it once too often. I'll not let this pass."

"Maybe," Brokaw said without interest. "Right now, just sit tight, with your hands in plain sight there on the saddle horn."

"We don't have to take this off him, Ollie," Shep Russell said then. "One of us can get him."

"Sure," Brokaw drawled. "And you'd like to be the hero that makes the first move, I take it. You'd die, Shep. You and Ollie, because I'd get you both before you could pull your guns. And there's Ross and his man. What do you think they'd be doing all that time?"

Shep glanced about the silent group and turned slowly for his horse. He kept his hands high, well in view as he climbed aboard.

"On the horn, Shep, like the others," Brokaw said with a careless wave of his gun.

Russell, placing one hand on top of the other, dropped them as he was ordered. Strove, finished with his chore of cutting out the Arrowhead stock, four in all, rode up. There were still a good twenty-five of Ross's beef in the jag.

"You can move out now, Ollie," Brokaw said. "Take your boys and get back on the job."

144

Godfrey, the seething fury turning him white, jerked his horse savagely around and started up the slope, the others trailing after him.

Ross got back onto his horse and rode in close, a smile on his lips. "Much obliged to you, Brokaw," he said. "Looked a little close there for a minute or two."

Brokaw nodded, still thinking there was a possibility, a remote possibility, that Ross could be Matt Slade. It hardly seemed likely, being Ann's brother, but you never knew for certain about anything. He decided then he would do some checking into the man's life.

"This will probably mean trouble for you with the Prestons," Ross said then.

"Don't worry about it," Brokaw murmured. "It's no stranger to me."

Ann came up to side her brother. She, too, was smiling, relief strong in her dark eyes. "I want to thank you, too. We owe you a great deal, Mister Brokaw."

She turned to her brother who was watching Brokaw with an odd half smile. "We've met before, George. This is the man I was telling you about."

Ross nodded. "I see," he said slowly. "Seems I'm indebted to you twice over. My thanks again."

He wheeled away, heading back to the stock where his rider was getting them under way. "Sometime ride over," Ann said, "and we'll try to thank you properly." She, too, swung away and followed after her brother.

Brokaw turned about and headed for the slope. Jules Strove was waiting for him.

"When you was doin' that namin' off there a while ago, how is it you didn't count me in?"

Brokaw said: "I'm not ringing in any man on trouble unless he wants it that way."

"Anytime," Strove said in careful, distinctly spaced words, "they's some sidin' to be took again' Ollie Godfrey and his bunch, just count me in. I'd take it as a right smart favor. Now, how about a bit of that chuck there in your saddlebags? I'm hungry as a ground squirrel with a sore tooth."

"Then I guess we'd better eat," Brokaw said with a broad grin.

CHAPTER
ELEVEN

Hugh Preston was angry. It showed in the grim, tight set of his jaw, in the glitter of his eyes, and the small spots of white on the drawn skin of his face. Ollie Godfrey had lost no time telling of the Ross incident and now, shortly after supper, Brokaw stood in the parlor of the ranch house, facing the rancher. Godfrey was there, a knowing smirk on his features. Cameron, as foreman, was present, also. And Darla. She stood quietly to one side, taking no part in the conversation, but the power of her presence was undeniable.

"Is what Ollie tells me a fact?" Preston asked in his quick, clipped way.

Brokaw shrugged. "Hard to say, not knowing what he's told you."

"That he had some rustlers red-handed on our range this morning. That you threw a gun down on him and made him turn them loose."

"Not rustlers. George Ross. I just stopped a murder."

"Killing a rustler is not murder," Preston came back. "I've been trying to pin something on that man and his bunch for months. And when we finally do, you spoil it. Whose side are you on, Brokaw? Theirs or mine?"

"As long as I'm drawing pay from you, I'm on your side . . . up to a point, and that point is cold-blooded murder. Which is what that amounted to this morning. As far as Ross is concerned, I don't believe he's a rustler any more than you are."

"You don't think!" Preston cried in exasperation. "You've been around here one week and already you know all things. What makes you so sure Ross couldn't be helping himself to my beef?"

"What makes you think he is?" Brokaw countered coolly.

"We had him red-handed," Godfrey broke in. "I reckon anybody would call that proof."

"He was going to cut out the Arrowhead stuff in that herd, if you'd given him a chance."

"You believe that?" Godfrey demanded.

Brokaw's hard gaze settled on the cowboy. "Ross was telling the truth. Any fool could see that."

Anger pushed at Godfrey's eyes and his face flushed slightly under its tan. After a moment he said: "He's just got you buffaloed. Him and that sister of his."

"Where were you when all this happened?" Preston asked, wheeling upon Cameron. "Why weren't you there?"

"Little hard bein' two places at one time," the old foreman said dryly. "You had me workin' up on the north range."

"You got opinions on this?"

Cameron wagged his head. "George Ross ain't no rustler. I'm plumb sure of that."

148

"He'd say that," Godfrey observed sourly. "He'd take Brokaw's part, no matter what. Him and Brokaw's real pally. Brokaw's stood for him two or three times."

"Nobody's got to stand for me," Cameron said defensively. "I reckon I can take care of myself."

The room was quiet, only the slow breathing of Cameron, harsh and rasping, being audible. Brokaw slanted a glance at Darla. She seemed completely beyond the argument, wholly disinterested, but Frank Brokaw knew that was a surface impression only. She was vitally concerned, and he had the feeling she had much to do with whipping Hugh Preston into the state he was in.

But Preston had cooled considerably. He stood in the center of the room, idly pounding one fist into the open palm of the other.

"Little use in crying over it now," he said finally. "It may be some time before we again have as good a case against Ross such as this one. But when we do," he added, lifting his gaze to Brokaw, "I want you to stay out of it. Let Godfrey, or whoever is handling it, alone. They understand the problem. Don't interfere."

Brokaw said: "Just as you say, but I'll not be a party to a murder."

Godfrey spoke up. "Maybe you'd better take my advice, friend, and move on. Maybe you ought to find yourself another job."

"No need for that," Preston snapped. "I want good men. Need them, in fact. You stay on the job, Frank, but do the things you're supposed to and don't get in the way when there's something you don't understand."

"All right, Mister Slade," Brokaw said, and watched the rancher's face.

Preston's glance swung slowly to him, a frown knitting his brow. "What? Slade? Who is Slade?"

Brokaw shrugged. "Slipped out. Used to know a man named Matt Slade. You remind me of him, I guess."

Preston seemed to be studying. He shook his head. "Can't recall hearing the name before. He from around here?"

"Farther east," Brokaw said, and turned for the doorway. Preston's expression looked sincere enough. But you could never tell about a clever man.

Behind him Cameron said: "If they's nothin' more, Mister Preston . . ."

"That's all," the cattleman said curtly.

Brokaw moved into the yard and came about, waiting for Cameron and for Ollie Godfrey. The foreman was close on his heels, but the cowboy made no appearance.

The foreman pulled to a stop beside him. "That danged Ollie," he grumbled in his deep voice. "Hightailin' it to Preston like that. Why didn't he come to me first like he should have?"

"Too big a thing for a foreman," Brokaw said with a dry smile. "Things like murder go to the head man."

"That's sure what it would've been had you let Ollie have his way. George ain't no rustler."

"I know that. But why does Preston want him out of the way so bad?"

"Not hard to figure. Preston wants that land and water, 'specially the meadows. And I figure there is a mite of personal problem there, too."

"Missus Preston?"

"Sure. Who else? I've caught them talkin' once or twice. She'd sure like to see the Rosses out of the picture, one way or another. And I reckon she'll have her way, somehow or another. She can do about what she wants with the boss."

"I'm believing that," Brokaw murmured. "You better keep your eye on Ollie. He wants that job of yours in the worst way and he won't stop until he gets it."

"I've been figurin' that," Cameron said in a tired voice. "Reckon I am gettin' a bit old for the job."

Godfrey came out of the house and stalked by, saying nothing, taking little notice of them. He struck for the barn, walking fast.

"Now, where you figure he's headed?" Cameron wondered, a light worry in his tone.

"To cool off, likely," Brokaw said.

Cameron thought that over for a moment. He shrugged. "Prob'ly right. If I know Hugh Preston, he gave Ollie a dressin' down for lettin' you get the drop on him and messin' up that deal this mornin'. You hittin' the hay now?"

"Not yet. Think I'll have a smoke or two first."

"Good night," said Cameron, and clomped heavily off to his quarters.

Brokaw watched him depart. The yard was silent and the only lights were in the cook shack and in the main house. Presently these, too, went out and the ranch lay

151

in the soft, silver glow of the main and bright stars. A horse blew wearily in the barn and a man's low-voiced curse rumbled from the bunkhouse for some cause or other.

Godfrey came from the stable then, astride the black stallion he generally rode. He came across the yard to Brokaw and halted, facing him at a distance of a half dozen feet. His features were stone cold and hatred burned in his eyes at slow flame. His right hand rested on the butt of the gun at his hip.

"I'm through talking to you, Brokaw. I told you it wouldn't be healthy for you around here. Now, I'm saying it no more. Get out. Get off Arrowhead and stay off. If you don't, you're a dead man."

Imperceptibly Brokaw had squared away in the half light of the yard. In a soft voice he said: "You backing your own talk, Ollie? Or is there somebody else that does it for you."

Godfrey stared, hard and pressing at Brokaw. Then he moved his shoulders slightly. "Don't be around here come night fall tomorrow, that's all," he said, and swung the black out of the yard.

Brokaw watched the man leave. There had been no idle talk in the cowboy's warning; it had been a genuine and solid threat, and, while he might never push Godfrey into drawing on him, Ollie had other means for getting the job done — Shep and Domino and several others, and a bullet in the back while he was riding across the range. From this time on he would have to watch his back trail.

152

He was far from sleep after that. He started across the hard pack, thinking back on Hugh Preston's reaction when he had deliberately called him Matt Slade. There had been no visible jar, no alarm leaping into his eyes or over his face. But a smart man would play it that way. He would be difficult to catch off guard, particularly if he were expecting something. There had to be a better way of testing Preston, something that would prove or disprove definitely whether he was Matt Slade or not. But if there was not, he still could force Preston back to Central City. That would be a final resort. He moved on by the bunkhouse, by the other sheds, and came to the grove at the edge of the clearing. Settling back against the thick trunk of a cottonwood tree, he drew out his muslin sack of tobacco, papers, and rolled himself a thin, brown cigarette.

She appeared before him so suddenly, so unexpectedly that he was momentarily startled. He stared at her, outlined sharply in the pale moonlight.

"'Evenin', Missus Preston," he murmured.

"I've been waiting for a chance to talk to you," she replied, stepping closer to him. She was wearing a robe drawn tightly about her slim body.

"You think this is a good place?"

"Makes no difference now," she answered. "I've run out of patience with Hugh. He's a silly, weak fool. I'll do better without him."

Brokaw glanced at her speculatively. "When he was known as Matt Slade, there was nothing weak about him."

"Matt Slade?" she echoed. "I heard you call him that before. Why? Who is this Matt Slade?"

"Maybe it's another name for Hugh Preston. I'd like to know for sure."

Darla shook her head. "He's never been anybody but Hugh Preston. I'm sure of that."

"You never heard the name of Slade before?"

"Not until you said it tonight."

Brokaw considered that in silence. Dead end. Maybe it was a blind trail after all, for who should know a man better than his wife, than the woman who had lived with him for years?

"But I didn't come here to talk to you about some Matt Slade. I came to see if you had reconsidered, if you had changed your mind about throwing in with me." She paused, eyeing him closely. "Brokaw, I need your help in getting what I want. Hugh's weak and it will take very little to get him out of the way. You saw how he acted about that affair with George Ross. If I had been Hugh, I would have killed you for spoiling a chance like we had. And so would have you. But that can be fixed. There'll be another time and we won't again slip up. You know better now and we'll have all of Double R to add to Arrowhead. It will be the biggest ranch west of the Mississippi. And the strongest and most powerful. We will control everything . . . even the politics of the territory. Brokaw, I'll be plain about it. I need you with me. Help me and I'll see you get everything you want."

Brokaw's glance was reaching beyond her, to the deeper shadows of brush a dozen yards away. Without moving his head he whispered: "There's somebody in the piñons across the way. Could be trouble. Turn and walk away from me, slow and easy, and, when you reach the other side of the feed barn, run for the house."

Darla did not move. There was no fear in her tone when she spoke. "Why? Why should I run from anybody?"

"You want Hugh to find you here? With me?"

"Why not? I'm finished with him. The sooner he knows about it, the quicker matters will come to a head."

Brokaw shook his head. "No, not yet. Better that you go. We don't want the rest of the crew to know about anything. Can't tell which way they might lean."

His words had no real meaning to him. He simply was striving to send her away. She hesitated for a long moment, as if that question might also be settled then and there. But she turned away finally and moved off, keeping to the deep shadows. Brokaw let a deep sigh run through his lips and then swung to the thicket.

"All right. Come out of there!"

There was no reply, no answering movement in the brush. Brokaw kept his eyes riveted to the spot where he first had seen the dim outlines of an eavesdropper. Hand near his gun, he called out again. There was no response. When he made a careful search some minutes later, he found no one, and so he returned to his pallet in the barn.

CHAPTER
TWELVE

Cameron was awaiting him that next morning. He stood just outside the cook shack, a puzzled, wondering look on his craggy features. Other riders moved by him, going in to breakfast. He stopped Brokaw with a lifted hand.

"Preston wants to see you," he said. "You get in some kind of trouble last night?"

Brokaw shook his head. "Not that I know of. Do I eat first?"

Cameron said: "No, he wants you first thing."

Brokaw pivoted on his heel and crossed the yard, a fine thread of warning running through him. The front door banged and he saw Ollie Godfrey leave, swinging to the left so as to not meet him. The cowboy flung a quick, triumphant glance over his shoulder and disappeared around the far corner of the building. Anger stirred swiftly through Brokaw. So that was it — Ollie Godfrey again. He was getting fed up with Godfrey, his patience wearing thinner, as one incident with the cowboy piled up on another.

He reached the side entrance and rapped. Preston's voice, high and strained, said — "Come in." — and he twisted the knob and entered. The room was flooded with lamplight and warm from the flames in the fireplace. Preston stood in the center, his face a mottled fury. A pistol was thrust into the waistband of his creased, woolen trousers. Darla, tall and cool with faint color showing high in her cheeks, was near the heavy library table, her fingertips drumming lightly upon its polished surface.

A strong caution laid itself upon Frank Brokaw. Here was trouble; here was something he had not anticipated, something that smelled mightily of a trap of sorts. He pulled to a halt in the big room and settled himself squarely on his two feet while the angle of his jaw stiffened.

"You sneaking saddle bum!" Hugh Preston burst out at once. "I might have known what to expect from you!"

Brokaw's gaze shifted to Darla. There was no explanation in her eyes, only a smooth detachment, a satisfaction in a victory that was beyond his understanding. He came back to the rancher.

"Seems to be something wrong here. Before you go any further, let's hear it. I'd like to know what it's all about."

"So you will know," Preston echoed, his voice lifting. "As if you didn't! You think you could get away with this?"

"With what?"

A spasm of fury wracked its shuddering way through Preston. "Don't play cozy with me, Brokaw! I know what you've been up to." The man's words reached a hysterical pitch and Brokaw, watching him narrowly, expected him to snatch at the gun in his waistband any instant.

Patience fled from Brokaw. "Get on with it, Preston. What's on your mind? I'm not standing here and listen to you rave much longer."

"Tell him! Tell him!" Darla suddenly cried, and began to weep.

"You'll stand there until I'm through with you!" Preston shouted. "Or I'll kill you!"

"Maybe," Brokaw replied evenly. "And maybe you won't. Point is, if you don't say what's bothering you, you may get your chance."

The rancher turned to Darla and laid his hand on her arm. "Never mind, dear," he said. "You won't have to be afraid any more." He wheeled back to Brokaw. "You're a cool one. But you don't frighten me any. You may look tough but I know your kind."

"So you know my kind. If that's all you wanted to tell me, then you've done it."

"I called you here to tell you to get off my ranch. And if I ever see you around here again, I'll kill you. I'll give my men orders to shoot you on sight. Understand that? You show up anywhere in this country and I'll put a bullet in your black heart. I should anyway . . . right now. It's a hell of a thing when a man's own wife can't be safe on his own ranch."

Brokaw's glance flicked again to Darla. She had been watching him closely and now she turned quickly away.

"Yes," Preston said, noting the exchange, "she told me. And if that isn't enough, you were seen by another member of the crew. You deny it? You deny you met up with my wife yesterday morning on the range? You deny you forced yourself upon her last night when she stepped out for a breath of air?"

Understanding came swiftly then to Frank Brokaw. Godfrey, somehow, had forced Darla's hand with Preston. And she had, in her desperation, swung all blame to him. It must have been Godfrey in the thicket last night. And now he was caught neatly in the squeeze.

He said: "Did she tell you that?"

"She did. And so did Godf- . . . one of the men."

"Let your wife tell me the same thing," Brokaw said then, looking at Darla.

The rancher swung to his wife. "Go ahead, dear. Tell him. Everything you told me."

Darla whirled around, placing her back to him. Sobbing, she said: "I didn't tell you all, Hugh. About the trip from town. The day you sent him to meet me . . ."

Anger blazed again across Preston's face. "Get out of here!" he cried. "Get out of my sight before I shoot you where you stand!"

Darla's wracking sobs filled the room. "Oh, Hugh, I'll never live it down. There'll always be the shame, and then, if he's alive, he'll talk, he'll tell other men . . ."

Brokaw, never taking his eyes from the rancher, said: "Don't touch that gun, Preston. You haven't got a chance."

Outside in the yard Brokaw could hear the cowpunchers coming out of the cook shack, their morning meal over. He heard the dull thud of hoofs as the wrangler brought up the horses, ready for the day's work, and turned them into the corral. But those things were subconscious, below the surface of his senses. He was thinking of Darla Preston; she had trapped him neatly, she and Ollie. He had played right into their hands. From the very start, it would seem.

"I'll take that chance," Preston murmured, coming around to face Brokaw. His eyes locked with the tall rider's and for a few moments held. And then fell away. A look of hopelessness crossed his face. "I can't do it," he said in a lost voice. "I couldn't kill any man."

A shrill cry wrenched from Darla's lips. The deafening blast of a gun in her hand rocked Brokaw. He saw an expression of surprise and then disbelief pass over Preston's agonized face. The man pulled himself to his toes, reaching up, twisting half around until he was looking at Darla, and the smoking pistol, again firing at pointblank range at Brokaw. It missed by inches and thudded into the wall. Brokaw leaped for her and the gun roared once more. Yells lifted outside in the yard.

"You've killed my husband!" Darla's voice went echoing through the house and out the open windows.

Brokaw struck her fully on and they went down in a crashing heap. He wrenched the gun from her fingers, then threw it into a far corner. Darla, screaming steadily, was like a writhing snake, pressed beneath his body. He slapped her soundly and struggled to his feet, dragging her with him. The yawning door to the hallway was before him. He half threw her into its cavern, slammed the door, and pushed a heavy chair against it.

160

"You murdered him!" her voice, muffled and insistent, came through to him.

Brokaw whirled into Preston's office. Fists were hammering at the side door. It swung open and the vague shape of a man was outlined there. He drove him back with a snap shot that thudded into the nearby door frame. He leaped through the office entrance and out into the yard. It was just breaking daylight and shadows were beginning to lift. Around the structure, on the hard pack, he could hear shouts and the pounding of boots. He circled the house swiftly, placing it between himself and the sounds.

Running lightly, he traveled its full length. At the end corner he paused. Faintly he could hear Darla, still imprisoned, screaming. She was making it look good. He smiled grimly. The whole plan was clear to him now. Darla would goad Preston into shooting it out with him. If both died, all would be well and good. If one survived, she would see that he did not leave the room alive and her story would be, in either event, that both had been killed in a gun duel.

Only Preston had failed to come through, even after so fantastic a tale as had been told him. So she had shot him, and then turned her gun on Brokaw. Even her failure to accomplish that had not stalled her clever, scheming mind. She had immediately cried murderer for all to hear and now he was a target for all their guns. They would be after him, hunting him down. She would see to that and with Ollie Godfrey at their head there would be no let-up until he was dead. Their only hope of safety lay in his death.

He laid a close survey on the bunkhouse, lying a short distance ahead. It was deserted, he was sure. All those who had not already ridden onto the range, to begin the day's work, would be there in the yard or in the main house.

Even at that moment, no doubt, they would be starting their search for him. He hurried across the narrow open space that intervened, reaching the north wall of the bunkhouse. He passed around that building, coming to its extreme southwest corner. If he could cross to the barn without being seen, he might gain entrance. And once inside that building there would be horses. If he could get astride his gelding, he would have a half chance of escaping. But there was little time. It was steadily growing lighter, and Ollie and the crew would be working closer.

He decided it was wiser to double back and go completely around the barn instead of risking the shorter, more open route. He was too likely to be seen running across the yard. He wheeled about and raced along the back of the bunkhouse. Cutting left, he went around the tool sheds and feed house and came to the grove where he had met Darla the night before. He heard a yell go up from the front of the house. Somebody had seen him.

He ran a long fifty yards through the brush, thinking it might draw them off, believing him to have taken refuge in the grove, and then cut left to the barn. The wide, double doors at the rear were closed, but there was a window, empty of glass, shoulder high above the ground. Without hesitating he launched himself at it.

He would have to take a chance on there being someone inside.

He gained the sill and pulled himself through into the gloomy, dim cavern of a building. A broad square of light marked the open doorway at its far end. He dropped lightly to the floor, still wary of somebody hiding in the deep shadows, and started forward, looking for the bay horse. Shouts were a running chorus in the yard, coming from all sides, it seemed. No one yet, apparently, thought he was far from the main house, believing that he was in the grove.

He located the gelding and his hopes dropped. The horse was not saddled and bridled and there was not time to throw on his gear. Two stalls farther along he found a buckskin ready to ride. One of the night crew rider's mounts, not yet relieved of its tack and turned into the corral. Without hesitating he stepped to the stirrup and swung up.

Wheeling into the runway, he walked the horse quietly toward the front doorway, gun in hand. He would have to break out at a fast run, counting on catching the men in the yard by surprise. And while they rushed to get their own horses, he would gain precious distance toward the hills to the west. He wished heartily for the bay; having a brief wonder if he should gamble the extra time it would take to get him ready. A voice, coming from the side of the barn, gave him his answer. He had run out of time — there was none left. The buckskin would have to do and that was not good, for he knew the horse was already dog-tired.

He reached the doorway and halted, settling himself in the strange saddle. The stirrups were too short and his knees stuck up awkwardly. He was lucky to have even found the buckskin, he told himself. Bending low, gun ready, he drove spurs into the buckskin's flanks. The little pony bolted through the door in a long, startled leap.

Ollie Godfrey was waiting for him.

Godfrey's gun blossomed red orange. Brokaw felt the burning shock of a bullet slap into his leg. He snapped a shot at the big cowboy. Godfrey staggered, his arm jerking back behind his crouched body. Brokaw drove another bullet at him, hastily, but he was having a hard time of it with the plunging buckskin, and the shot went wide.

Yells broke out. One or two guns flatted in the early morning air, but he was already out of the yard, going into the grove, running hard for the distant bluish haze of the Sierra Diablos. The buckskin, thoroughly frightened by the crash of gunfire, was going at his top speed and Brokaw let him have his head.

Hooking the reins over the saddle horn, he punched the empty cartridges from his gun and reloaded from his belt. When this was done, he shoved the .45 into its holster and turned to the wound in his leg. The initial anesthetic of shock was beginning to wear off and sharp pain was making itself felt. The hole was about halfway between hip and knee, bleeding freely from both openings. The bullet had made a complete passage, going through the fleshy part of his leg at a slightly upward angle. Luckily it had missed the bone. He

164

glanced down at the saddle skirt. A fresh scar showed where the lead had emerged, struck a solid surface, and glanced off into space.

He ripped his handkerchief into strips, making two pads that he bound against the puckered holes. The hard running of the buckskin made the job impossible insofar as a tight bandage was concerned, so after a time he gave it up. The pads would stay, perhaps, until he could reach some sort of shelter. Then he would pause and do the job properly.

He crossed completely through the grove and broke into the open prairie with the bulk of the mountains still miles in the distance. Twisting about in the saddle, he threw a glance at his back trail. No pursuers were yet in sight. He came back around, growing a little giddy from the swinging motion. Shaking his head to clear away the mists, he cursed softly. A little nick in the leg like that should not give him much trouble. He must be getting soft.

The buckskin began to tire, to slow down. His long, reaching gallop dropped to a run, then to a fast trot. He was blowing hard and flecks of foam came back on the wind and plastered against Brokaw. He was trembling badly, and Brokaw realized he was good for little more at his present pace. He pulled the little pony in. He could take no chances on his going down now. The horse would have to last, to carry him at least until they gained the shrouding safety of the brushy hills, for Brokaw knew he was in no condition to walk.

He looked again over his shoulder. He was still alone on the vast roll of flat land. But it would not be so for much longer. Arrowhead riders would be pounding through the grove on fresh horses, even at that moment. They would soon gain the edge and break into view, and, when they caught sight of him, they would ride in earnest. He let the buckskin idle along, trying to conserve his strength. He was not blowing so badly now, but he still shook from his earlier exertions. Brokaw would need every ounce of strength and speed the horse had when Arrowhead's men began to close in.

It came to him then with jolting suddenness. Hugh Preston dead — and he would never know for certain now if the rancher was actually Matt Slade. The blast from Darla's gun had stilled Preston's lips and he would take his secret, if he had one, into the grave with him. And if he was Slade, the chance to clear Tom Brokaw's name was gone forever. But should he assume that was true, that the rancher had been Slade? Should he give up the search now, satisfied in the knowledge the man had received his just rewards and mortal punishment at the hands of his wife? Or should he go on looking for a shadow, as he had been, being suspicious of every man he met who fit a vague description, who had money to spend freely?

The description, he had discovered, fit a multitude of men. He could think of a half dozen who fitted the same general outline besides Preston. There was George Ross, the man called Domino, Ollie Godfrey — even Abel Cameron except he likely was too old. The money narrowed it down considerably, but even that could have vanished in the past few years, and Matt Slade could be a poor man again.

But that would all have to wait for a time now. He was a hunted man himself, one with a murder charge hanging over his head. A posse was at his heels, thirsting for his blood, and Darla Preston, now a powerful and ruthless force in the Scattered Hills country, was driving them after him. She would never let them rest until she had him lying at her feet; he alone was the sole remaining threat to her safety.

Where should he go? In the blazing heat of his escape he had not given it any consideration other than the immediate need for reaching the mountains and hiding there. But he could not remain there for long. There was the matter of food and water and care for his leg. And Ollie Godfrey and Arrowhead would search every foot of it. He might escape them for a time, but not for long. He thought then of making his way to Westport Crossing, to Ben Marr and telling the sheriff what had happened. He shook off that suggestion with a curling of his lips. He had no proof to back his own statements and who would the law believe — the bereaved widow, or the word of a stranger? The law was not the answer.

The sun was warming to his back. He reached for the canteen hanging at the saddle. Shaking it, he found it to be about half full. He took a swallow, rinsing his dry mouth thoroughly before he permitted it to drain down his throat. There should be water available in the mountains, but he must take no chances. He would have to hoard his small supply until he located some.

He pivoted again in the saddle, more slowly and with greater effort. He supported himself with one hand on the saddle's horn, the other on the cantle while giddiness slogged through him. The posse was in sight now, well out of the grove and streaming across the prairie. They were no more than dark blobs, but coming fast, and taking on definite shape and outline with each fleeting second. He twisted back around. The mountains were closer now. Not over two miles at the most. He patted the buckskin's sweaty neck in a dazed, addled way, unaware that he yet clung to the horn to stay in the saddle.

"I'm real sorry, old horse," he muttered.

He peered ahead through the mistiness flooding his eyes, selecting a cañon opening onto the prairie that would afford sanctuary. He was heading almost directly into the largest, and the approach was gradual and not steep. Brokaw settled himself lower on the buckskin, trying to brush away the weariness that was overtaking him. He kicked his spurs into the horse and the game little animal broke into a gallop. Pain wrenched through Brokaw at the first solid shock of the horse's coming down, but he clamped his jaws tightly and hung on. After the initial spasm the pain flattened out into a solid, running string of fire coursing all through his body. His eyes began to glaze under it all, but he hung on.

The posse was a distant scatter of riders when he leaned forward and urged the buckskin to greater effort. A half mile from the cañon's mouth the horse began to flag, leaning heavily to one side as he favored his left foreleg. Brokaw pushed him cruelly onward, up the lifting slope, every step of the animal's adding to and multiplying his own misery and pain. But mere pain was beyond him now; there was only the necessity to reach the sheltering depths of the cañon.

He was vaguely conscious of finally getting to the top of the grade, finding himself on a sort of ridge that ran for miles in either direction along the foot of the mountains. A shallow valley lay between and he drove the fading buckskin down into it. Behind him a gunshot echoed, a signal of some sort, apparently, for the posse was far out of range.

More from instinct than any conscious thought, he swung left and traveled along the floor of the swale until another cañon broke off to his right. He guided the limping horse up this, looking desperately for a place into which he might turn and remain safely hidden. At every hand small gullies fed into the main wash but these he avoided, knowing they were dead ends and would form a trap from which he might not escape. He heard another shot, off to his right. The posse had crested the ridge. They would pause there, uncertain, trying to find the direction he had taken. A few more minutes would be recovered.

A large arroyo cut off at an angle to his left. Without hesitation he turned into it, barely conscious that it curved back toward the prairie. It was thick with cedar and oak brush, and the buckskin labored with every step of the climb, plunging along like a horse in deep

169

snowdrifts. Brokaw knew the sounds of their passage were loud but there was no help for it. There was no turning back now, no seeking an easier, less overgrown trail. He pushed on, clinging to the saddle horn with both hands.

The buckskin scrambled up a steep bank and came upon a ledge, too beat to go farther. Brokaw hung for a long minute, and then slipped from the horse's back, catching himself with his hands. And for another long minute he clung there, upright against the heaving pony. This was the limit of travel, the stopping point for both himself and the valiant horse.

He released his grasp and stood for a moment, swaying slightly. His head had cleared somewhat as the pain lessened when the buckskin stopped plunging beneath him. He would have to make some sort of stand here. He did not know how well hidden he was; he might be out in the open for all he knew, but it would have to be all right. There was no reserve left in either him or the horse. Suddenly the starch went out of his knees and he sat down, his legs simply folding beneath him. The buckskin shied away, too tired to move far, and coming to a halt a half dozen steps distant. He was still breathing heavily, sucking for wind with his head low between his legs.

Brokaw dragged out his gun and tried to focus his eyes toward the end of the cañon. That would be the point any searching posse member would first appear, he figured. It was an indistinct, fuzzy blur and all things seemed to be moving in a slow, swirling motion. He shook his head savagely, trying to halt the confusion.

170

He heard a shout then. It seemed far away, far to the north. But he could not be sure if it actually was in the distance or only seemed so to his reeling senses.

CHAPTER
THIRTEEN

The sun was his friend. It reached down from a clean, steel sky, wringing from him the little moisture left in his fevered body. It stirred him restlessly on his rocky pallet, twisting him first one way and then another. It popped beads of sweat from his brow that rolled off his dark face, and down onto his chest. But finally it awakened him.

It was near noon, he judged. He had lain there for three, maybe four hours. Somehow the posse had not yet discovered him and that in itself was some sort of miracle.

His head throbbed sullenly, and a rivulet of fire traced up and down his injured leg like a continuous flash of jagged lightning. He was kitten weak from the loss of blood and lack of food. When had he last eaten? Last night? Or was it the night before that? It was all mixed up and confused in his mind.

He turned his head slowly, and caught the buckskin a dozen paces away, cropping at the scanty grass on the ledge. His teeth made hollow, clacking noises as they closed and the saddle leather creaked with his movements. Brokaw wished he had loosened the cinch. It would have eased the tired horse. The fact of the matter was, he recalled, he had not been able to do much of anything.

He pushed himself to a sitting position. His mouth was parched and he glanced to the canteen hanging at the saddle. He got to his feet then, moving unsteadily and favoring the leg. It had stopped bleeding sometime during the hours he had lain on the bench, but at his first attempt to rise he felt it start anew, a warm, sticky feeling.

He hobbled awkwardly toward the horse that watched him with tired, suspicious eyes. *All I need*, he thought, *is for that damned horse to spook*. But the pony remained where he stood, too tired to shy off, and Brokaw eventually reached him. He hung again to the saddle, appalled by his own inadequate strength while all things swam in front of his eyes.

The water in the canteen was hot. But it was wet and it eased the stiff dryness in his mouth and throat. The buckskin, smelling water, turned to watch. He took his bandanna from around his neck, poured a quantity of the liquid on it. Working his way to the pony's head, he rubbed the animal's quivering lips and nostrils, managing to squeeze the cloth dry in his mouth. The horse made loud, sucking noises and tried nervously to get more, but it was all Brokaw could spare for the time. He rubbed the pony's neck and eventually quieted him down.

His head had cleared again and this aroused a vague worry in him. He was too keen, too alert, and he was fearful he was not far from fever delirium. He groaned. He could not allow that to happen now. It would be dangerous to remain there on the ledge overly long. Luck had been with him so far, but it would not last. The posse, failing to find him in an area they knew he had entered, would backtrack and search more diligently. He hobbled to a slab of granite and sat down. He must think calmly and act rationally.

Deliberately he built himself a cigarette, rolling it with hands that were far from steady. He spilled considerable tobacco, but finally it was made, and after the first few drags he felt some better. He decided the thing to be done next was to look after the wound. Blood was oozing from the lower hole, the exit of Godfrey's bullet. The pads he had made and crudely fastened in place were now stuck to the skin, and it took several painful minutes before he got them loose. This done, he refolded them, placed them over the angry vents, and bound them tightly in place.

It was not the best treatment, hardly any treatment at all, but it was the best he could do. He could not continue to lose blood indefinitely. What he needed was hot water, and something with which to cleanse the wound. He would have to find a ranch house.

A faint halloo drifted to him through the hot, still air. It came from below, from the prairie. He was instantly alert. Gun in hand, he moved off the slab and made his way to the edge of the shelf, going the last few feet on his hands and knees, to avoid being seen by anyone scanning the slope — or looking upward. Reaching the lip, he found he was on a sort of eyebrow that overlooked the entire side of the mountain and afforded

174

a balcony-like view of the flat land below. On his belly he let his gaze run out over the prairie.

A half dozen horsemen were gathered below, holding some sort of council, it appeared. He immediately picked out Ollie Godfrey, the bandage of his left hand standing out startlingly white at that distance. He could also make out Shep Russell and Buckshot Martin and Domino. The other two riders were not distinguishable. Off to the right a single horseman was loping leisurely toward the group. They were in no hurry. They knew he had little time left, while they had plenty. He was wounded and could not go far on a tired horse.

The lone rider joined up, unrecognizable to Brokaw, and for a long ten minutes the meeting held. It broke up with the men fanning out in different directions, but all pointing into the flanks of the Diablos. One, however, soon pulled away from his companions. He dropped into the swale lying between the ridge and the foot of the mountains and rode northward. Brokaw watched him thoughtfully, coming to the conclusion that his task was to find a trail that led to the top-most point of the mountains from which he could look down. And from there Brokaw knew he would be spotted.

He could remain here no longer, that became immediately clear. They would find his hiding place now, without question. They would work deeper into the cañons from below and watch from above, then in the end they would flush him out and shoot him down. He crawled back to the slab, ignoring his throbbing leg and the faintness that now seemed to be continuous.

He threw a glance along the rim of the hills towering above him. He was about a third of the way up. It appeared rough and steep — he doubted if the buckskin could make it. The north and the east were closed off to him, with posse members swarming all through it. The only route open was to the south. That would take him farther from the riders so eagerly probing the draws and arroyos. It would also take him off Arrowhead land and onto the range owned by George Ross. He gave that brief thought, thinking he might head for that point. But it would not be wise. Failing to find him in the mountains, Double R would be the first place Godfrey would look.

But beyond the Double R there would lie other ranches. If he could reach one of those, he could obtain aid for his leg, food and water for the buckskin and himself.

He got to his feet too quickly; the motion sent a wave of nausea flooding through him, and he sank back onto the slab of granite. He waited out what seemed a long time, then tried again, moving with more deliberateness now. This attempt succeeded and he half walked, half crawled to the waiting horse. He was breathing hard when he reached the animal and he clung to the horn and cantle for support, gathering his strength to climb aboard.

It was then his flagging mind remembered the pony had gone lame back on the prairie. It was like a blow from the edge of a board and it left him sagging against the horse, limp with despair. But after a minute the will to fight came back and he sank to his knees. He patted

176

the buckskin's foreleg until the horse lifted it for his inspection. He examined the hoof, hopeful it was nothing more serious than a wedged-in pebble.

There was no stone visible and he let the hoof fall. A tendon, maybe. He felt the pony's leg, but it seemed firm and straight, with no swelling. Nor did the horse try to pull away. He struggled to think clearly, to remember. Had it been the left side, the left foreleg? Or was it the right? It was the left, he was positive. What then was wrong?

He raised the buckskin's leg again. There was the faintest chink of metal. Loose shoe! Feverishly he looked it over. He found the fault, a bit of gravel lying between the hoof and shoe. He searched his pockets for his knife, opened it, and dug about until he flipped out the offending bit of stone. The shoe was really loose, but he feared to do anything about that. Hammering at it with a rock would start a noise bound to be heard by someone.

Then he led the buckskin to the slab of rock, thus giving himself a three-foot lift above the ground. Standing upon it, he crawled into the saddle, the effort sending his senses rocking back and forth in his head, like loose shot in a bucket. He managed to find the stirrups, resting his weight heavily upon his right leg until he was settled. The pony started up the faint game trail leading off the ledge.

For the first hour or so he managed to hang grimly to consciousness as hunger and pain, thirst and weakness slogged through him relentlessly. The buckskin plodded slowly on, guided only by the narrow path itself. Finally it became too great an effort for Brokaw to hold his eyes open and he sagged forward in the saddle. Only the rigidness of his wounded leg, and the death-like grip on the horn kept him from falling.

Off to the south, a far distance from the hills, Ann Ross pulled her spotted horse to a halt and watched thoughtfully the slow, graceful glidings of the vultures. There were four of the huge birds circling high above the mountain's slope, dipping, rising, weaving in the noonday sky like leaves caught in the vagrant whims of a summer wind.

They were still high which meant their intended prey was not yet ready, not entirely dead. But they knew, they always seemed to know, possessing some uncanny sense of doom. She wondered about their victim. It could be a calf lost from its mother, but that seemed hardly likely. It was too far up the slope. It could easily be a steer down with a broken leg, or possibly a horse or deer or some other unfortunate animal, pulled to the ground by a lion. Or it could be a man.

Her mind came to a full halt on that thought. She was marking strays, locating the singles and jags of stock drifted from the range and lost in the brush and thickets. Later she would report the locations to her brother and he, or another of the men, would go after them. It worked out well; it saved the crew from spending so much time poking around the edges of the range. There never was a big enough crew on the Double R, it seemed.

178

Ann frowned. It was late to start for so distant a point as the mountain slope where the vultures circled in their tireless way, but the thought that it might be one of their own beeves down and the almost certain possibility that more would be nearby was pressing her sense of duty. It would be well after dark when she reached the ranch and George would be angry and worried. He had been that way ever since that affair with Godfrey and the other Arrowhead riders. But she doubted if any Arrowhead men would be that far south. This was, she thought, Double R land and the slope of the mountain still lay in it, or very nearly so.

She put her pony to a slow gallop, crossing the prairie at an easy, ground-gaining pace. Thinking of Hugh Preston's crew, she wondered again about Frank Brokaw. She had made no headway with George in her efforts to get him hired on as foreman. At first he had seemed mildly interested, telling her he would think about it. Then, yesterday morning after the incident with Ollie, he had come to a decision. They had talked about it on their way back to the ranch.

"That's the man I was telling you about," she had said. "The one that stepped in and stopped Ollie."

George had nodded his head. "Brave man. Maybe a little on the fool side, but plenty of nerve."

"He's probably looking for a job right now. Preston will never keep him after Ollie gets through talking."

"We couldn't afford him."

"Why? He'll likely work for regular wages. I'll bet Preston's not paying him any more than that."

"If he would work for nothing," George had said with emphasis, "we still couldn't afford him."

"But why not?" she had persisted, somehow disappointed and not at all understanding his reasoning.

"Hiring him would be like waving a red flag in Hugh Preston's face. We'd have Ollie and that bunch of hardcases down on us before dark. It would be inviting trouble and we've got all we can handle along that line now."

"I doubt if they'd try much with him around."

"Maybe not," George had said. "But there's little we would gain. We might even win out, but there'd be mighty little left of the Double R to crow over. You can figure on that."

It had ended there. Ann had recognized the futility of saying more, at least for the time, but she had not given up. She remembered the way Brokaw had sat there, his strong face so still, so calm, yet so certain in its purpose. He possessed that quality of speaking low and in such a way that men did not hesitate to comply quickly with his orders.

She reached the first outcropping of rock and halted, lifting her glance to the sky, to the black-winged silhouettes biding their time in fluent flight. They were nearer than she had thought. Whatever it was they watched was somewhere on the side of the slope, about where the trail laced across its rough terrain.

She touched the pony with her knees and they moved ahead, beginning the ascent. It was country she had been over many times in the past, and she turned now for a steep break-off at the end of the long, parallel ridge. Here she could double back and reach the path. The pony made it easily, scarcely breathing hard from the effort, then she headed him around for the north.

In another half mile she reached the larger timber, pines and a few spruce. A screen of brush to her right shut off the prairie from view, but she was paying little mind to that, to the thought she might now be on Arrowhead range, and therefore in danger. Her glance was on the buzzards, almost directly overhead at this point.

She reached the cañon where the spring lay, shallow and cool, in a small clearing and halted there. She allowed her horse to drink while she probed the slope ahead with careful, painstaking eyes. She could see nothing but the glistening, heat-slapped rocks and the gray-greens of the underbrush. And there were no sounds, her approach having stilled even the forest's wildlife. Urging her pony away from the water, she continued on, knowing she could not be far off now. If whatever it was the vultures watched was on the trail, she would find it soon. If it lay off and hidden in the welter of draws, thickets and tangles of brush and rock, it might take some time to locate it.

She climbed a steep stretch, the horse stumbling a bit on the weather-polished stones of the trail, and rounded a bulging shoulder of rock. Her breath caught momentarily. There, dead ahead, was a man on a horse. He was folded forward in the saddle, head sunk deep into his chest. The worn buckskin horse he forked was

181

near collapse, standing with legs braced wide apart, half on, half off the trail.

Ann studied the exhausted pair for a full minute, something about the man stirring her memory. The buckskin, sensing the other horse, lifted a tired head and took a faltering step. The rider's hat fell off and rolled away in an awkward, loping fashion. Ann gasped. Brokaw! The man was Frank Brokaw!

A wild sort of fear raced through her, something she had no immediate understanding of, or explanation for. She saw then the dark crusted blood along his leg. This had been his reward for helping them yesterday morning. With a little cry she leaped from the saddle and ran to him, snatching up his hat as she passed by it. She placed her hand under his whisker-stubbled chin and raised his head. His eyes were closed, sunken. Stricken with a nameless fear, she unbuttoned the top of his shirt and laid her hand upon his heart. She felt the strike, slow and light. He was still alive.

It was a long quarter mile back to the spring. She unhooked the reins from the horn, seeing he was safe in the saddle, anchored by his own locked hands and stiff muscles, then led the buckskin down the trail. Her own pony fell obediently in behind, and minutes later they were in the cool glade where the spring bubbled noisily from beneath its overhung, moss-covered ledge.

She could not hold the buckskin when he got his first smell of the water. It was all she could do to keep Brokaw in the saddle when he lunged by her, but somehow she accomplished it. While the horse sucked his fill, she pulled Brokaw's feet free of the stirrups, pried loose his hands, and dragged him from the saddle.

His weight was solid, more than she bargained for, and he struck the ground hard. A groan escaped his cracked lips, but his eyes did not open. She laid him out in the shade on the cool grass, then turned to the buckskin. It took her leather belt applied as a whip to drive him away from the stream, but it had to be done. She could not allow him to founder himself. There would be need for him later.

She filled the canteen with water and let a small amount of it trickle into Brokaw's parched mouth. Making a compress of her folded handkerchief, she soaked it and draped it across his forehead. He seemed feverish, but not in too bad a condition. He stirred when the coolness of the cloth penetrated the fog in his mind and he opened his eyes. But he was not conscious, she knew that. A dozen questions were crowding her, but there was no time to think of them now. That leg would have to be attended to. And then food, from her own lunch that, luckily, she had not paused to eat. And more water, as soon as he could drink.

CHAPTER
FOURTEEN

He became conscious first of the coolness on his brow. He had been going through a sort of dream, in reality a fever nightmare in which he visualized himself again at Arrowhead, standing completely alone in the empty yard near the main house. Darla Preston faced him from the doorway, calm and beautiful as she leveled the pistol at him.

Involuntarily he cried: "Darla!"

He was aware then of someone bending over him. The indistinct, blurred face of a woman. He knew it was a woman because of the halo of hair. And he thought then it was Darla, that it had not been a dream at all, that she had shot him down and was preparing now to finish the job. He tried to squirm away, struggling with little strength. Light fingers began to stroke his face, his cheeks, feeling odd and remote, as they traced across the wire-stiff whiskers along his jaw.

He managed to bring his eyes into focus, trying to separate the nightmare from actuality, the true events of the last hours from the confused ramblings of his mind. The posse! Where was the posse? What had happened to them? And where was he — where was this place? It was dark and cool. Could he be back at Arrowhead, a prisoner? The last thing he could recall was climbing onto the buckskin and starting along the mountain trail. What had taken place since that moment?

Vision came into his eyes. Ann Ross was beside him, a soft smile on her full lips. Her face was turned half away as she looked out over the prairie. Somewhere in the stillness a squirrel was scolding and he could hear the steady, contented cropping of a horse as it grazed. The late afternoon sunlight filtering down through the screen of trees glinted upon Ann's dark hair and deepened the tan of her skin, giving it a sort of golden softness. He noted with a start that her shoulders were bare; she wore no shirt and the curve of her breasts was visible above the undergarment she wore.

He lay there quietly wondering at the strangeness of that. He felt much better. The pain in his leg had subsided to a dull ache and the few hours sleep he had garnered had worked wonders for him. Ann, he decided, must have accidentally stumbled upon him as he came down the trail. But he could not recall their meeting, nor how he had arrived at the shady place where now he lay.

Wry humor moved through him. "If this is heaven and you're my special angel, I reckon I'll like it here fine."

She turned to him at once, quick light springing into her eyes. "How do you feel?"

"Better. A lot better."

She felt the press of his gaze on her shoulders and read the question in his eyes. "I had to have bandages for your leg. The shirt was all I could think of."

185

There was no embarrassment in her tone, no false modesty. Only a matter-of-factness that bespoke her practical side. It was something that had to be done and so she did it.

"I thought you might lend me your jumper," she added after a moment.

Brokaw glanced to his leg. His Levi's had been slit from knee to thigh and the wound was bound tightly with clean, white cloth. A strip of lacy, eyeleted trim stuck out from beneath one fold.

"I'll bet that's the fanciest bandage ever a man wore," he commented with a grin.

With some effort he raised himself to one elbow. She helped him get an arm out of the jumper, reverse the process, and pull free the other. The jacket was twice too large for her and she became momentarily lost in it, but this she finally whipped by tucking the tail, woman-like, into her skirt's waistband. It didn't look quite so large then.

During that he lay back, watching her pull and tug until she was satisfied with it. When she turned back to him, he said: "How did you happen to find me?"

She said: "Buzzards. I saw them circling and figured something was down. Maybe one of our own steers. I never thought it would be you."

That brought an immediate alarm to him. If she had spotted his whereabouts by such means, others would have noticed the birds and arrived at the same conclusion. "Where are we now? How far from where you found me?"

"About a quarter of a mile. If your buckskin had gone on just a little farther, he would have got wind of the water and brought you here himself."

"He was about done for."

"And so were you," she murmured. She was waiting for him to make some explanation of his condition, of why he had been there in the Diablos, of what had happened at Arrowhead. But, woman-wise, she was patient; he would tell it of his own accord, if indeed he wanted her to know about it. She would ask no questions. "You didn't wake up during all the time I was working on you . . . not even when I poured the whiskey in the bullet hole to clean it."

"Whiskey?"

"I found a little in a bottle in your saddlebags."

"Not mine," he said. "I borrowed the buckskin in a hurry."

"I see," Ann replied but she pressed it no further. "Are you hungry? There was a lard bucket and a sack of coffee grounds there, too. The coffee has been used so many times it's about worn out, but I made you some anyway. It's ready if you want it."

He had not thought about food, the surprise of the first moments being so great, but now he realized how hungry he was. "Go mighty good," he said.

Ann moved away at once to where she had built a small fire of smokeless dry twigs. Brokaw managed to pull himself to a sitting position. His head spun a little and he was short of breath when it was done, but it was not too bad.

She brought him the tin of coffee. He tipped it up and drank it empty without pausing. She was right; it was weak as rain water but it had some strength and it tasted good. Almost at once the hot liquid made him feel better. She handed him two cold biscuits and a few strips of dried beef.

"Part of my lunch. I wish there was more."

He ate it without question, and, while he was doing so, Ann took the lard tin and refilled it from the stream. She set it back over the fire and replenished the fuel. He watched her busy herself at the task, but as he slowly became his old self and reason once again took hold, worry began to haunt him. It was growing late; he had been there on the mountainside almost the entire day and the posse could not be far off. They had not given up. Godfrey would never face Darla with the word that he had escaped. And he did not want them to find Ann with him.

He said: "We should be getting out of here."

"As soon as it's dark," she replied over her shoulder.

"Have you seen any riders around?"

She shook her head. "Nobody has been by here and I haven't seen any on the slope. I did hear a yell but it was to the north."

"How long ago was that?"

"Over an hour, at least."

Brokaw glanced to the sky, arching blue and clear above the Diablos. The sun was beginning to swing low, not far above the highest ridges and peaks. It would be a full two hours until dark, he judged.

"We've got to get out of here," he said. "That posse can't be far off."

He started to rise, turned restless by the urgency and danger, found he had miscalculated his strength, and settled back on the ground. In an angry sort of helplessness, he shook his head.

Ann, watching him, said: "What posse?"

He thought he detected a lifting change in her tone, sort of disappointment, or perhaps it was dismay. He said: "Ollie Godfrey . . . Arrowhead."

He told her then of the events at the ranch, leaving out a large portion of the story, giving her only the pertinent details. She listened in silence, the tan oval of her face serious. When he was finished, she said: "So Hugh Preston's dead and Darla owns Arrowhead. That's what she wanted. I knew it would happen someday, but I thought it would be Ollie she used."

"I think that was the way it was planned. Ollie forced her hand for some reason."

Ann was silent, still busying herself with the fire. Without turning to him she said: "What does Darla mean to you?"

"Mean to me?" he echoed. "Nothing, except that I need her to clear my name of a murder."

"Is that all? Do you know you called out to her, cried her name while you were still unconscious?"

Brokaw's dark face was still, puzzled. He shook his head. "I can't explain that. I don't know what would make me do something like that."

"Perhaps it was just a dream," Ann murmured.

"A bad one," he said with grim humor.

"And she means nothing to you, no more than being a witness who can prove your innocence of Hugh's murder?"

"That's all. Once I get clear of Ollie and his bunch, I'm going back after her and make her tell the truth about it."

"You think, for a moment, she will do that? She has too much to lose. She'd never do it."

"Not willingly, of course. But I'll force her to somehow. She made her use of me, now I'll have my time."

"She will keep Ollie on your trail until he runs you down. And they'll kill you."

Her voice broke slightly and Brokaw threw a sharp glance at her. But she was not looking at him, her eyes lost in the dancing flames of the fire.

"First they'll have to catch me," he said in a reassuring voice. "And as to the killing, I'll have a little to say about that."

After a time she said: "Did she send for you to come and work on Arrowhead?"

"No," he said, "I came looking for a man named Matt Slade. I thought Preston might be him, and still think it might be so." He remembered then his suspicions regarding her brother, George Ross.

"This Matt Slade, you must want to find him very badly."

"I do," Brokaw said. He told her then of Central City, of his father and mother, and of the endless trails he had followed. When he had finished, he came up to a sitting position, again restless and anxious to be moving. He managed to get to his feet and tried a few experimental steps. The jagged pain returned at once but he kept at it, feeling his way, favoring the injured member.

Ann watched him, saying nothing. Her eyes were dark and deep and filled with thought, her face serene and still. There was a tenderness about her as she viewed his first painful efforts, but she was wise enough to offer him no help, knowing he would not want it that way. He hobbled out of the small clearing, finding a length of branch that he converted into a cane. He paused at the trail where he could see beyond the slope, out onto the prairie now fading into pale gold under the lowering sun.

She said: "This search for Matt Slade has almost cost you your life. It may yet before it is done with. Why don't you forget it?"

"Forget it?" he echoed in a surprised voice. "How can a man forget such a thing as that?"

"Vengeance is a bitter thing," she murmured. "It will affect and color you as much as it has Matt Slade. And if you catch up with him, what good will it do? It won't bring back your mother, or change what has already happened to your father. It can only result in a death, yours or his, and at best it can end with your becoming an old, broken man, hating everything and everybody and each day of your life."

"You think a man like Slade deserves to live? To enjoy what he has taken at the cost of two lives?"

"I think he likely has already paid for what he did in many ways. He could be dead himself and you might be wasting your life chasing a shadow, but if he is not, his days cannot be pleasant ones, not with that memory in his mind."

He came slowly back into the clearing, back to where she still knelt by the fire. The coffee was beginning to boil and she added another handful of twigs to the flames, extracting all the remaining strength from the overworked grounds.

"It sounds simple, the way you put it," he said, settling down beside her. "But it's a thing I could never do. I live for one thing . . . to settle with Matt Slade. I'll find out, somehow, if Preston was Slade. If he wasn't, then I'll start to look again."

A small sigh passed through Ann's lips and her shoulders fell slightly. She lifted off the tin of coffee and placed it on the ground near him. "There is little of anything you'll do until that leg is healed."

"I'll manage," he replied. He took up the coffee, offering it first to her. When she shook her head, he tipped it to his wide mouth and drank it down. He said then: "How far are we from open ground?"

"Two miles, more or less."

"It will be dark by the time we reach it if we start now. We'll have to chance their seeing us on the trail. I've a sudden feeling we had better get out of here."

She rose and stamped out the fire. That done, she walked to where the buckskin and her own pony were picketed at the edge of the clearing. Brokaw, back on his feet once more, checked the loads of his gun and shoved it back into the holster. He could not remember replacing the spent cartridges, but somewhere along the way he had done so. A sort of reflex action, he guessed. He was feeling much better, the combination of hot drink, rest, water, food, and his own immense vitality coming to his rescue.

Ann moved up with the horses and he prepared to mount. He forgot the leg momentarily, shifting his weight so that it fell fully upon it. It gave way as a solid sheet of pain swept through him. He staggered back, coming against Ann. He threw out his arms to catch himself and her arms went around him, steadying him, and for a moment they stood that way, locked in embrace.

A sudden gust, wild as spring wind, went through Frank Brokaw. He dipped his head downward and crushed his mouth against Ann's lips for a breathless, sweet space of time. She did not resist, did not pull away. And then some of her calmness touched him and he released her. He took a short, half step back, his eyes serious as he studied her face.

She met his gaze straight on, the whisper of a smile on her lips. "Don't regret that," she murmured softly.

He shook his head. "A thing I'll never do."

For a moment they stood there, two people fully aware the first time of each other, and their own deep emotions — and being unafraid. But the urgency of time was pressing hard at him. He turned again to the buckskin.

Pulling himself into the saddle, he waited for her to mount and take the trail ahead of him. His own horse, rested, fed, and no longer harried by thirst, dropped in behind Ann's spotted pony willingly enough. The first flush of recovery had passed with his extra efforts and Brokaw was again feeling the drag of his wound and the loss of blood.

But he made no mention of it. Riding was painful and at each step of the buckskin, bracing itself with stiff knees on the downgrade, fire rocketed through his body. When Ann glanced over her shoulder to see if he wanted a minute's rest, he shook his head.

The going was slow along the slope. Brokaw tried to maintain a sharp watch to the rear and along the sides of the mountain, but the brush was thick and he had little success. And he heard nothing that caused any alarm. That assured him somewhat; a single rider, much less a whole posse coming along the rocky trail, would be certain to set up a loud clatter. It was just closing dark when they came to the end of the path and broke onto the prairie. He saw then the first indication of the posse.

A lone rider. He was high on the mountain, sitting his horse on a ridge that circled the highest peak and furnished him with a broad, far-reaching view of the entire country. Brokaw spoke his warning to Ann and they halted, watching the silhouetted horseman with close scrutiny. After a long five minutes the rider swung about and struck northward. They followed him for a short time, then he was gone from sight, dropping behind a bald knob that thrust up from the piling rocks.

"Did he see us?"

Brokaw shook his head, easing himself to one side of the saddle. "Hard to say. My guess is that he did. We were pretty much out in the open that last half mile.

But if he did, we've got the advantage of time. He's got to come down off that mountain and get word to the others. That will take an hour, even more."

"We can get to the ranch before then," Ann said.

Brokaw said: "No, Ann, I'm heading on to the west. I'll make the next place and hole up there until my leg gets better. Then I'll be back."

At once she said: "That's foolish! It's more than fifty miles to the McCausland's, the nearest ranch. At least a hundred beyond that to the next town. You're in no shape to travel even the fifty."

"I can't hang around here. That's what they are figuring I'll do."

"You can come to our place, to the Double R. If just for the night. Then I could tend that leg properly and you could get some rest. Besides, you'll need supplies."

It made sense, Brokaw had to admit. But if Godfrey found him at the Double R, the wrath of Arrowhead would descend with full force upon Ann and her brother.

He said: "I can't do it, Ann. There would be no end to the trouble it would cause if Ollie found me there. And if that rider spotted us, it will be the first place they will look tomorrow."

"That's just it," she said. "Spending the night won't be dangerous for us. And you'll be gone early in the morning. Anyway, we're only guessing that Ollie's man saw us and we won't be seen *now*. It's too dark."

Brokaw again considered the man on the horse etched against the night sky. Perhaps he had not seen them. And he would be a long time getting down the mountain, if he had.

He nodded. "All right. We'll ride to your place and talk it over with your brother. If he's agreeable, I'll stay the night and be glad for your kindness."

He saw her face lift suddenly to him, as if his words had hurt her, as if they carried far less meaning than she had hoped. But she said nothing. She wheeled her spotted pony around and together they started for the ranch.

CHAPTER
FIFTEEN

They rode into the yard at Double R shortly after 9:00p.m. George Ross met them, a tall figure holding a lantern above his head. He was worried and he showed it on his face. He stopped shortly before them, recognizing Brokaw.

"Ann, where the hell have you . . . ?"

"Help me, George," she broke in, sliding from her saddle. "He's been shot."

Ross set the lantern on the ground and moved up to assist her, placing his hands under Brokaw's shoulders and pulling him off the buckskin as gently as possible. Brokaw, breathing hard from the pain, grinned his thanks to the rancher. And in that same moment the inconsistency of his own feelings struck him. Here he was accepting the aid and hospitality of a man he had come to suspect as one he might be forced to kill!

"What happened? Who shot him?" Ross asked of Ann.

"Ollie Godfrey," Ann replied. "We must get him inside where I can doctor that leg."

With Ann on one side, Ross on the other, they started for the house. Ann sketched briefly the things that had taken place at Arrowhead and, later, on the slope of the Diablos.

At the doorway George Ross halted. In the pale moonlight his face was sharp, his gray hair pure silver. He said: "You shouldn't have brought him here, Ann. You know that. This man means trouble."

Ann lifted shocked eyes to her brother. "But he's hurt. Don't you understand that . . . he's been shot, probably as a result of what he did for us. We can't refuse to help him!"

Ross changed his attention to Brokaw. "Nothing personal in this," he said, "but we haven't much show against Arrowhead, once they take it in mind to crawl us. I have to try and avoid all the trouble I can with them."

Brokaw nodded but he was having his own thoughts about the matter. Was George Ross truly afraid of Godfrey and Arrowhead — or did he have another reason for not wanting him around?

But Ann was involved and she could get hurt if Arrowhead struck. And he would not have that, regardless of cost to himself. Before he could speak Ann said: "It will be just for tonight. Long enough to get him ready to travel. He plans to leave early in the morning."

"Makes little difference," Ross answered. "When Ollie and his bunch can't find him, where will they look first? Right here, of course. They know there's no other place he could go."

"He's right," Brokaw said then. "This is no good, Ann. Help me back to my horse and I'll move on."

"No," Ann said in a flat, determined voice. "You will do no such thing. You'll stay here until I can get that leg dressed. We can do that much . . . even if we are afraid of Arrowhead!"

For a moment George Ross said nothing. Then: "You're right of course, Ann. Maybe it's time to stop running from Arrowhead." He turned to Brokaw. "Forget what I said. You're welcome to stay here until you're ready to travel."

Brokaw saw pride move into Ann's eyes, as if she was glad her brother had finally stopped and was at last going to face up to his trouble. They helped him on into the house and to a back bedroom. Her own, he guessed, judging from the bottles and other feminine gimcracks on the dresser. He sat down heavily on the bed and lay back, dead beat from the ride.

"I'll stay here a short while," he said, brushing at his eyes. "That's understood."

"We'll see," Ann murmured, and left the room.

He came awake minutes later to her touch. She was removing the improvised bandages from his leg. A low table had been dragged up to the bedside and a pan of steaming water, several medicines, and a supply of fresh, white bandages lay upon it. George Ross, his face expressionless, stood quietly in the doorway.

Ann smiled at him, softly and sweetly, when she saw his eyes were open. She continued to work, washing the wound with the hot water, swabbing it with some sort of fiery disinfectant that caused him to stiffen and squirm a bit, and then salving it over with a cool ointment. Finished, she got to her feet and set the table back out of the way. Brokaw struggled to sit up. At once she turned to him, pressing him down into the comfort of the bed. "Not yet. Not until you've had another hour's rest. And something to eat."

From the door Ross said nothing, but the tight lines of his face reflected his thoughts and the worry in his eyes was undeniable. Again Brokaw had his wonderment at the man's true reason for nervousness. Was he actually afraid of Godfrey and Arrowhead — or did he fear to have Brokaw around?

He then said: "It's no good, Ann. My being here. I won't stay and cause you trouble."

"We've had it before," she said lightly. "More of it will be nothing new."

"Not the kind Ollie will bring this time," Brokaw said. "And I won't have you hurt because of me." He swung his attention to Ross. "If you'll stake me to a sack of grub and a canteen of water, I'll pull out of here."

Ann was looking at him, her eyes stricken. Her shoulders went down with their despair and she shrugged in a hopeless, tired way.

"It's the only sensible thing to be done, Ann," Ross said.

"There's no sense to anything," she replied. "No reason, at all."

Ross wheeled away, going to fill Brokaw's needs. Brokaw came to a sitting position and worked himself off the edge of the bed. He crossed to where Ann stood and took her gently into his arms.

200

"You must understand this . . . I can't be found here. I can't let myself cause you trouble."

"It wouldn't matter, as long as we were together," she murmured in a faraway voice.

"I know, but can't you see I could never live with myself if something happened to you, because of me. It's the best that I leave now but I'll be back. You can depend on that. Nothing is as important as seeing you again."

"Not even your looking for this Matt Slade?"

He waited out a long minute, studying his answer to the question. He said finally: "I can't answer that, Ann. I don't know yet. It's a problem that will take some thinking. But I will come back."

"How can you be so sure?" she cried, holding tightly to his arms. "How can you be sure you'll reach the next ranch or town? That Ollie won't follow you and hunt you down? Against him, in the condition you're in, you wouldn't have a chance."

"I don't kill easy," Brokaw said with a short laugh. "You know that now. And believing that you will be here, safe and sound, waiting for me, will give me that much more strength."

"I'll be worried, wondering . . . ," she began.

Brokaw bent down, checking the words with his kiss. For a long minute he held her close, soaking in the feel of her body pressed against his own, the softness of her, the freshness of her hair. He was having his own great difficulties in comprehending the moment; why, when he had found the solitary thing in his life that really mattered to him, he was being forced to leave it. But it would not end here; he would find a place to hide, to rest and recover from his wound, and then would be back. Nothing could keep him from Ann.

"You'll be here?" he asked softly.

"Until you come back," she replied. "No matter how long it takes."

From the doorway George Ross said: "Everything's ready, Brokaw. Grub in your saddlebags. Canteen is full. You got plenty of ammunition?"

Brokaw stepped away from Ann. "I've plenty."

Ann turned from him and he followed her to where her brother waited. Ross said: "We'll help you to the barn."

They crossed the yard to the large, sprawling building. The ranch was still, almost deserted it seemed. Ross, seeing the wonder on Brokaw's face, said: "Crew's all out on night herd. Three men's all we hire."

They reached the barn and entered. A lantern hung inside the wide, double doors, throwing a fan of yellow light down the runway and into the first stalls. The buckskin, saddled and ready to travel, munched at the manger, getting in a final meal. Farther along, Ann's spotted pony waited to have his gear removed.

Ross said: "I hung a little sack of grain for the horse on the horn. You may need it before you get where you're going."

Brokaw had turned away from him, from Ann, a breathless sort of feeling closely akin to fear racing through him. He moved deeper into the first stall that had been made over into a tack room for the gear and other equipment. His eyes were upon a saddle racked upon the bar, a saddle with heavy silver trimmings, with silver dollars mounted along its skirt just as he had been told they were. He reached out a hand. It trembled slightly from the emotion that ripped through him as he ran his fingertips over the deep, handsome tooling. There was no doubt. He came back around to face them.

"Who," he asked in a tight voice, "does this belong to?"

CHAPTER
SIXTEEN

In that suspended fragment of time following his question Frank Brokaw remembered many things: the way George Ross had reacted to his presence at the ranch, his anxiety to have him out of there and on his way, the swiftness with which the rancher complied with his request for food and water. But most of all he recalled Ann's words back in the shaded glen on the slope of the Sierra Diablos: vengeance is a bitter thing. It will affect you as much as it will Matt Slade. It would be better forgotten, she had meant. Was she thinking of her own brother when she spoke those words?

He could not believe it; he would not. But he faced them both with a stiff mask that covered the torment raging through him. Ann — the one woman who had, in a lifetime, come to mean more than a passing fancy to him — the sister of a man for whom he had searched and sworn to kill . . .

"Yours?" He pushed the question at Ross.

Ann said: "No, it's mine."

Brokaw stared at her unbelievingly. "How can it be yours?"

"It was given to me. Why?"

Relief began to flow through Brokaw. "Who gave it to you?"

She gave him a wondering look. "Is it so important? It was given to me by a man who once worked here. As a birthday gift. And then he left, went away."

"Who," Brokaw said again, "who gave it to you?"

Ann said: "Ollie Godfrey."

Godfrey!

A sigh passed through Brokaw's lips and the tension slipped from his taut frame. The alleviation that came with the knowledge that it was not George Ross, not Ann's brother, was like the lifting of a dark and heavy cloud from his mind, almost overshadowing the fact that at last he knew who Matt Slade was, that the trail had come to an end.

Ann was regarding him with disturbed eyes. "What is it, Frank? What's wrong?"

"Ollie is Matt Slade," he said.

Realization came swiftly to Ann. Her eyes spread into wide circles of surprise as the meaning and its implications grew upon her. "But you can't . . . not in your condition . . ."

Brokaw shook his head. "This changes it all. But I'll not wait here for him. I'll find him and have it over with."

George Ross spoke for the first time in many minutes. "What's this all about? Who is Matt Slade?"

"No time to explain it," Brokaw said, moving toward the stall where the buckskin waited. "Ann can tell you later. You say Ollie worked here for a time. Know much about him?"

"Only that he came with a lot of money," said Ross. "Wanted to buy in with Hugh Preston but Hugh wouldn't hear of it. I think they were acquainted before they came into this country."

Ann had turned and now blocked his way. She looked earnestly into his face. "I won't let you do it. You won't have a chance. At least wait until tomorrow, until we can go into town and get Sheriff Marr. He'll listen to you."

Brokaw shook his head. "It's too late for the law, Ann. They'll have nothing to do with it."

"But if we all go . . ."

"No," said Brokaw in a final tone, "it's my affair. I'll handle it my way."

He pushed her gently aside, moving toward the buckskin. There was a sudden rush of horses in the yard.

A voice yelled: "Ross!"

Brokaw came around in a swift, circling motion. Ann clutched at his arm, staying him. Ross gave them a quick glance and moved to the doorway. He pushed half the double width open a yard or so and stepped outside.

"Yes?"

There was a sound of horses coming nearer. Ollie Godfrey said: "You've overstepped yourself this time, Ross. You've got a killer hid out here somewhere. I want him. Either you turn him over to me, or I'll burn this place down to find him. Make your choice."

Brokaw said: "Get out of the way, Ross. This is my fight."

The rancher did not turn or make any sign he had heard. To Godfrey he said: "Who says he's here?"

"I do," another voice spoke up. "Watched him and that sister of yours ride off the mountain and head this way."

Brokaw thrust Ann roughly back into the stall. "Stand back, Ross!"

"No!" Ann cried. "You can't go out there! You can't stand against them all!"

"What'll it be, Ross? You trottin' him out or do we come after him?"

Ross said — "You'll have to come after him." — and drew his gun. He snapped two quick shots at the riders and leaped back, dragging the door closed with him. There was a blast of gunfire. Bullets splintered through the planking of the barn and thudded into the thicker boards of the stalls. Ross, caught in the runway, staggered against the wall and dropped to one knee. Ann cried out and Brokaw, heedless of his leg, leaped to the man's side. With Ann's help, he dragged him into the shelter of the stall.

"You damned fool!" Brokaw said in a furious, savage voice. "This is no quarrel of yours!"

Ross smiled up at him. "Always has been but I didn't want to face up to it. Should have called Ollie's hand a long time ago."

"Stay with him," Brokaw said to Ann.

He moved back into the runway. More bullets splatted against the doors and front wall of the structure. He kept low, pointing for the small window that offered a vantage point from which to shoot.

Reaching it, he looked out. A half dozen riders were wheeling about in the yard. They had started a fire and flames were licking at the sides of the main house and the wagon shed. A man, a torch blazing in his hand, came toward the barn, his intent plain. Brokaw leveled a shot at him. The cowboy dropped the torch and folded out of the saddle, his horse shying off into the darkness beyond the flare of light.

An answering hail of bullets came after that, setting up their cracking sounds and thudding into the thicker timbers.

"There any other way out of here?" Brokaw called over his shoulder. He was firing regularly, keeping the riders clear of the barn on its front side. It would not be long, he knew, until they began to concentrate on the other walls. There would be no holding them then.

Ann said: "No. Only the windows and they're too small and high. Like the one you're at."

"We've got to get you out of here. And your brother. He needs a doctor bad." He turned back to the shattered window. "Ollie!"

Godfrey's answer came back to him. "Yeah? That you Brokaw?"

Brokaw said: "Ann's in here. And her brother is with her. He's been hit. Hold your fire and let them out. You've got no cause to hurt them. It's me you're after."

"Ross shot one of my boys there a minute ago. And there's a few other things I've got to settle with him."

"Let Ann pass then."

"I'll not go," Ann said firmly from the depths of the stall. "I won't do it!"

Godfrey's voice said: "You'll all come out together, or none of you'll come out. Makes no difference to me."

A shot followed his words. A bullet smashed into the remaining glass of the window, showering Brokaw with stinging slivers. The main house was a roaring inferno. Flames were leaping high into the night, casting weird, dancing shadows in the yard. Somewhere a dog barked hysterically and riders whipped in and out, shooting at will, paying little heed to Brokaw's single gun. He was at a disadvantage, his scope for shooting hampered and limited. Maybe, if he could get into the loft, he would be in a better position to keep them at a distance, away from the structure.

He emptied his gun at the Arrowhead riders and ducked back into the stall where Ross and Ann were. The rancher was sitting up, holding one hand to a stain on his left breast. His face was gray, the muscles sagging but his eyes burned with a feverish brightness.

"I'll give you a hand in a minute," he said as Brokaw dropped beside him.

"How bad is it?"

Ross said: "Hard to tell. Lots of blood but we've about got it stopped."

Brokaw was not hearing him. He was getting his answer from the rancher's drawn features and the slow drag of his breath.

Ross said: "I think I can manage it now. Just help me up."

Together they got him to his feet. He leaned back against the stall, grinning. Sweat lay across his face in an oily shine, and the effort to stand was costing him dearly. He drew his gun and pointed it at the door.

"I'll hold the fort," he said with a pretense of jocularity. "You two, take a look in the back of the barn for another door. Seems to me like there's one there somewhere. Near the northwest corner. Look behind all that stuff that's piled there." He paused, coughing a little. "Stay close to the wall," he cautioned.

Brokaw was watching him with narrow suspicion. Ross caught his gaze and gave him a brief, hard grin as Ann slipped out of the stall. "It's all right," he murmured. "You look after her."

Ann tugged at his arm and he followed her into the runway. The yelling and shouting had increased outside and there was a thump, as something struck the front of the barn and fell to the ground. Probably a torch. They kept close to the stalls, past the second one in which the buckskin stood, the third that sheltered Ann's little pony. The runway turned in a right angle. "I can't remember seeing any door," Ann said. "That will be the corner George spoke about."

Together they crossed to the point indicated by Ross, piled high with old wagon wheels, harness, broken tools, and other such items.

"Take an hour to move all that stuff," Brokaw observed. "And we don't have that kind of time. We've got to figure another way out."

A yell lifted near the front of the barn, near the doorway. Brokaw wheeled and hurried as best he could toward the runway. The door was swinging back, opening onto the confusion and glare of the yard.

George Ross, astride Brokaw's buckskin and leading Ann's pony was momentarily outlined blackly against the lurid background. The gun in his hand roared, and the buckskin leaped into the open, dragging the pony after him.

"George!" Ann screamed, and started for the doorway.

Brokaw seized her arm and pulled her to one side as guns cracked and bullets sang by them. Ross, bending low in the saddle, weaving uncertainly as he fought to stay on the buckskin, cut sharply right through the smoky gloom. A chorus of yells sang out as Godfrey and the others caught sight of the plunging horses. Another welter of gunshots ripped through the night and then all went thundering across the yard in pursuit.

Understanding came then to Frank Brokaw. He took Ann's hand in his own. "Come on!" he cried, and started down the runway.

They reached the doorway and paused there. Brokaw threw a searching glance over the yard. It was empty, all the riders having given chase to Ross. To Ann he said: "Any more horses around?"

"In the lower corral," she replied in a dazed, wooden voice. "To the left."

They slipped through the doors into the open. The front of the barn was starting to burn in three or four places, and they were compelled to swing out a distance from it to escape the rapidly climbing flames. Moving as fast as he could, they reached the corner of the doomed building and turned. The corral was still a long distance away, a hundred yards at least, but it was beyond the fire's glare.

A spatter of shots came from the south, from the direction taken by Ross. They seemed to be some distance away, indicating the rancher had drawn Arrowhead's riders off considerably.

Ann at his shoulder said: "George did that . . . made a break for it to pull them off so we could escape."

Brokaw said: "Yes. He knew he didn't have much chance of making it with that hole in his chest, so he chases us off into the back of the barn and then runs for it."

"Why did he take my horse, too? That slowed him down. He would have had a better chance if he hadn't done that."

"I guess he figured Ollie would think it was the two of us. He knew George was shot. When he saw two horses come out of the barn, he probably thought we were all that was left. That's what your brother wanted him to think, otherwise he would have left some men to watch the yard."

They reached the corral. A half dozen horses milled nervously about, sticking into a bunch in the far corner. In the dim starlight, aided only slightly by the fire's glare, they caught up two of the animals. Both were haltered, but there were no saddles available.

"Can you manage it bareback?" he asked.

Ann nodded. "But what about you? How can you ride with that leg in the shape it's in?"

He said: "Don't worry. It seems a lot better. I guess a little exercise is what I needed."

212

She was looking away from him then, back toward the burning Double R. He knew she was thinking of her brother. "Don't worry about him," he said, laying his arm around her shoulders. "It was the way he wanted it. The last thing he said was for me to look out for you."

"He was the kindest man I ever knew," she said, and began to cry softly. But at once she checked herself. Brushing away the tears with the back of her hand, she said: "What do we do now? We can't stay here. Ollie and the rest will be back when they see they've been tricked."

"Can you ride to town?"

"If that's what you want me to do."

"Good. Get Ben Marr and bring him to Arrowhead. I'll be waiting there for you."

She studied his face for a moment. "Will that be wise? Won't Ollie go there, too? And the rest of the Arrowhead riders?"

"Maybe," Brokaw replied softly. "But you get Marr and bring him out. I want him to hear Darla Preston's confession."

He helped her mount, and, when she was seated, she leaned down and gave him her kiss. "Be careful," she murmured, and rode off into the darkness.

CHAPTER
SEVENTEEN

It was well after midnight when Brokaw reached Arrowhead. The ranch was a silent cluster of darkened buildings except for the main house, where the windows of the front room showed their squares of yellow light. He pulled up in the deep shadows on the north side and slid wearily from his horse. It had been a long and painful journey, one that did his injured leg no good.

He stood for a time in a pool of blackness, formed by a spreading cedar thrusting its branches against the starlight, and let the stiffness fade from his muscles and a measure of life work back into the wounded leg. Walking was a difficult task and this worried him. He had no plan, having given it little thought until this moment; there was only purpose — force Darla Preston to clear his name, then settle with Ollie Godfrey. Darla would be in the house now, alone. Godfrey would come later.

Moving quietly and with involuntary slowness, he crossed the narrow intervening ground and reached the corner of the house. He followed along the wall until he came to the door leading into Preston's office and there he paused, praying that luck was with him, that the door would not be locked. He placed his fingers on the knob and with infinite care, twisted.

The slab panel opened without sound. Gathering his faculties, he stepped inside, pushing the door, but not closing it, fearing the snap of the catch. He threw his glance into the parlor. The back of Darla Preston's head was partly visible above the thick roll of one of the leather chairs. She was alone, as he had suspected she would be, alone and awaiting Godfrey to return and tell her Brokaw was dead, that the Double R was gray ashes blowing in the wind, and George and Ann Ross were finished.

He moved a step closer to the portièred archway separating the office from the front room, still unsure as to his best course of action. He came to a sudden halt, hearing the rapid drum of a horse coming into the yard. It came to a sliding halt near the rail and a moment later a man's boot heels beat a tattoo of approach. Darla had risen from her chair and stood now facing the door, her face stilled by expectancy, lamplight spilling over her blonde hair, turning it yellow gold.

The door swung back and Ollie Godfrey came in. A wide smile was on his mouth, and, as he came to a stop just inside the room, he brushed his hat to the back of his head, giving him a young and reckless appearance.

"It's done with!" he said. "Finished."

"Brokaw's dead? And the Rosses?"

"We got Ross in the barn. Brokaw and the girl made a break for it. We went after them, the whole bunch of us. Chased them for miles. When I saw the girl's horse with an empty saddle, I turned around and came back.

215

It'll be just a matter of time, a few minutes maybe, and they'll have Brokaw."

"But you didn't see him dead?" Darla pressed.

"Not exactly but he didn't have a chance. Don't worry about it."

"You should have stayed there until you knew for sure," she then said, anger sharpening her tone. "I don't like things only half done."

Godfrey crossed to her and threw his arms around her shoulders. "I've told you, there's no need to worry about it. Brokaw's out of the picture. Now we can go ahead."

Darla pushed him away, falling back a step or two. She was not satisfied and it showed in her face. Trusting no one but herself, she had utterly no confidence in the promise of things done, only in the actuality.

Godfrey said: "The boys will be here soon. They'll tell you it has all been handled, just the way we wanted it. It's all ours now, sugar . . . Arrowhead and any part of the Double R we want. We can go right along and do what we planned. I'll ride to Santa Fe tomorrow and get my money from the bank, and then we'll be partners. Partners in the biggest ranch in the country."

Brokaw stepped from behind the heavy folds of the curtains, coming to a solid, square-shaped stance in the open archway.

"No, Ollie. Not tomorrow, not ever."

Godfrey spun about, surprise blanking his face and dragging down the corners of his mouth. Darla whirled

216

with him, throwing a hand to her lips to choke back a cry.

"You said he was dead!" she shrilled. "I knew you would slip up somewhere!"

Godfrey had recovered from his shock. A sly grin crossed his face. "Song's not sung yet," he murmured. "There's still another verse."

Brokaw said: "Don't fool yourself, Ollie. This is the end of the road for you. I've hunted you from one end of the country to the other. You'll not get away from me now."

"I can try," Godfrey said.

"Anytime you're ready."

Darla said: "I'm glad you're not dead, Brokaw. I'm glad you didn't let them kill you. It proves what I've thought all along. You're the one man I can depend on. Our deal still stands."

Brokaw was hearing only words, only sound. His eyes were on Ollie Godfrey, watching that man with a close and narrow surveillance.

"You hear? You and I will be the partners. We'll own Arrowhead and everything else we want, just like I have said before. We will control this part of the country."

Darla's voice was a near hysterical drone. Ollie Godfrey had slipped into a half crouch, his hand spread-eagled and poised above the gun at his hip. There was no smile on his face now, only a frozen grimness.

"Kill him, Brokaw. Kill him and get him out of our way. And then I'll swear you didn't shoot, Hugh, that it was him . . . that he did it and then ran outside."

Brokaw saw the break in Godfrey's eyes, that slight tip-off that telegraphed his intentions. His hand swept up his gun and he fired. Godfrey's own weapon crashed. He felt the solid wallop of the bullet, like a blow from a massive fist, somewhere high up on his right breast. He shot again at the buckling shape of Godfrey, dim and wavering in the boiling smoke and through it all Darla's voice was a high, shrilling scream overriding all else. And then he felt himself falling backward. He clutched at the portières, hung there momentarily, until the cloth ripped and gave way, and he dropped heavily to the floor. He remembered nothing else.

They found him that way, lying half in the parlor, half in Hugh Preston's office, the heavy drapes all but covering him. There was Ann, Sheriff Ben Marr, Cameron, and Jules Strove. They carried him into the bedroom and made him comfortable while Strove went to Westport Crossing for the doctor. Ann, not waiting, dressed the ugly wound and gave it the care it needed.

Godfrey was dead, shot twice. Darla Preston, her mind giving away under the fierce pressures that lashed it, broke down and told Marr all he wanted to know and Frank Brokaw was a free man. And there had been letters in Ollie Godfrey's pocket that cleared up the matter in Central City.

"Your daddy's a free man, son," Ben Marr told him. "Things in these here letters from Missus Preston to Ollie prove he had nothin' to do with the bank robbery. Reckon it proves somethin' else, too. Ollie had a mite of

218

conscience after all. Looks like he wrote her to send your ma some money to tide her over, 'a little of the ten thousand gold.' Her letters says she sent it, but I reckon we won't ever know if she did or not."

A deep peace had settled in Frank Brokaw. He was seeing Ann sitting close by and thinking it was all over, that the long trail had ended and there were no dark shadows in the background or waiting in the future. There were new things to talk of, things like a trip to Leavenworth and getting a harmless, fine old man released to their custody, the farm in Kansas that was waiting to be worked, or perhaps it would be the rebuilding of the Double R.

It was good to dream of the days ahead. Good to make plans. It was especially good to know he would be making them with Ann.

Acknowledgments

"Ben Sutton's Law" first appeared in *Truth at Gunpoint: Western Stories* by Ray Hogan (Five Star Westerns, 2004).

About the Author

Ray Hogan was an author who inspired a loyal following over the years since he published his first Western novel, *Ex-Marshal*, in 1956. Hogan was born in Willow Springs, Missouri, where his father was town marshal. At five the Hogan family moved to Albuquerque where they lived in the foothills of the Sandia and Manzano Mountains. His father was on the Albuquerque police force and, in later years, owned the Overland Hotel. It was while listening to his father and other old-timers tell tales from the past that Ray was inspired to recast these tales in fiction. From the beginning he did exhaustive research into the history and the people of the Old West, and the walls of his study were lined with various firearms, spurs, pictures, books, and memorabilia, about all of which he could talk in dramatic detail. "I've attempted to capture the courage and bravery of those men and women that lived out West and the dangers and problems they had to overcome," Hogan once remarked. If his lawmen protagonists seem sometimes larger than life, it is because they are men of integrity, heroes who through grit of character and common sense are able to overcome the obstacles they encounter despite often overwhelming odds. This same grit of character can also be found in Hogan's heroines, and in *The Vengeance of Fortuna West* (1983) Hogan wrote a gripping and totally believable account of a woman who takes up the badge and tracks the men who killed her lawman husband by ambush. No less intriguing in her way is Nellie Dupray, convicted of rustling in *The Glory Trail* (1978). One of his most popular books, dealing with an earlier period in the West with Kit Carson as its protagonist, is *Soldier in Buckskin* (Five Star Westerns, 1996). Above all, what is most impressive about Hogan's Western novels is the consistent quality with which each is crafted, the compelling depth of his characters, and his ability to juxtapose the complexities of human conflict into narratives always as intensely interesting as they are emotionally involving.